CW01084769

I WAS A
TEENAGE SPY

Paul W Robinson

CANDY JAR BOOKS · CARDIFF
2021

The right of Paul W Robinson to be identified as the Author of the Work has been asserted by him in accordance with the Copyright, Designs and Patents Act 1988.

I Was a Teenage Spy © Paul W Robinson 2021

Editor: Keren Williams
Editorial: Shaun Russell
Cover by Martin Baines

Printed and bound in the UK by
4edge, 22 Eldon Way, Hockley, Essex, SS5 4AD

ISBN: 978-1-913637-49-1

Published by
Candy Jar Books
Mackintosh House
136 Newport Road, Cardiff, CF24 1DJ
www.candyjarbooks.co.uk

All rights reserved.
No part of this publication may be reproduced, stored in a retrieval system, or transmitted at any time or by any means, electronic, mechanical, photocopying, recording or otherwise without the prior permission of the copyright holder. This book is sold subject to the condition that it shall not by way of trade or otherwise be circulated without the publisher's prior consent in any form of binding or cover other than that in which it is published.

— PROLOGUE —

It was a rainy night in Tangier. The month was July. It had been a steamy seventy-five degrees all day. The night was warm, wet and humid. The secret agent drew up to the kerb outside the casino, emerged gracefully from the Aston Martin DB6, and threw the keys, wrapped in a ten dirham note, to the parking valet. He turned up the collar on his Burberry raincoat and strode purposefully along the wet pavement towards the night's entertainment. Would it include a woman? Who could say? It was the kind of night when anything could happen.

The secret agent had just completed a difficult and dangerous mission. He was still recovering from the physical and mental effects. His leg still ached, and the fresh scar across his shoulders pulled as he walked. He paused for a moment and looked around the old town with unseeing eyes as he reminisced. He would never forget Olga. He remembered her red lips, the warmth of her body, the feeling of her heart, pounding…What a pity he had been forced to leave her. Ah well. He shrugged. There would be other women.

The secret agent felt that he had earned some time off and a little relaxation. People around him hurried towards the bright inviting doorway up ahead, its garish lights reflected in the wet pavement. Or, broken by the gaming tables, they trudged back to their cars, oblivious of the warm, heavy rain.

The secret agent mounted the steps and entered the casino. The air was blue with smoke; it reeked of tobacco, money and nervous sweat. A potent mix. He shook the rain off his hat and raincoat, which he handed to the checkout girl at the cloakroom. She was a dark little thing, petite and pretty. She gave him a warm smile. Tall, slim and handsome, in a piratical way, the secret agent's clothes fitted him like a second skin. He wore a dinner suit with black bow tie, an outfit which he carried off with nonchalant ease.

With narrowed eyes, like chips of pure blue ice, he surveyed the room. He noted the patrons with a mere passing glance, except for one. A beautiful blonde was watching him with a frank, open, inviting gaze. She had the kind of voluptuous figure that men dream about, and an appealing, luscious, smiling red mouth. Her huge blue eyes were fixed on him over her glass as she sipped her cocktail. He sat down next to her, and waved a waiter over; he—

'—Oi! Dilly Dream! Wakey-wakey! I *said* what do you

want?'

I climbed out of the shattered wreck of my fantasy. I looked around, red-faced. I saw to my horror that two of the worst bullies of my acquaintance were in the café, on this rainy day in July, the first day of the school holidays. They were sniggering at my discomfiture.

'Erm c-coffee!' I stuttered. I always stuttered. 'W-with milk, no sh-sugar.' I could hear them taunting me, ridiculing my stammer as I put my head down and tried to ignore the mocking laughter. It was one more humiliation in a long progression; one more miserable day in my miserable existence.

Then, one night, it all changed…

CHAPTER ONE

A Stone Dropped in a Stagnant Pool

'Please?' she asked. It was just two days after the embarrassment in the café.

'Please!' she repeated. She made it sound more like an order than a request. But anyway, how could I resist that pretty face, those huge green eyes, and that lovely voice?

'All right,' I faltered.' Erm, g-get under the bed. I'll shut the w-windows...'

I shall never forget that summer night. It was the night that changed my life forever. I was seventeen and three quarters; I had just finished the first year of sixth form. It was 1967, the so-called 'summer of love'. Not for me it wasn't...not so far at any rate!

It had been a very hot June. Now that the summer holidays had finally arrived of course, it had turned into a cool and wet July. It was raining that night, but it was still warm enough that I was sleeping with the windows open, which is how it all began...

I should explain some things at this point. My name is Williams, Philip Williams. I lived in a council house in a small village called Dokesley. That means 'raven's meadow'. It was mentioned in the Domesday book; as far as I was concerned, it was still stuck there!

The only entertainment in the area was the local pub, which I avoided like a plague pit. There was one shop in the whole place, run by old Mrs Ewell at the other end of the village. Apart from that, there was the church and that was it.

Otherwise it was a half hour bus ride – there were four buses a day – to the local town of Westford, and the one cinema for miles around. I spent a fair amount of my limited cash there. I loved films, spy films in particular. My favourites were the Bond films, but I watched anything, *The Ipcress File*, *The Italian Job*, *Carry On* films, anything.

Dokesley was in a mining area in the North Midlands and was surrounded by fields, farms and woods. The nearby colliery –otherwise known as 'the pit' –provided half of the employment opportunities. The other half was provided by the farms. Neither career appealed to me.

I mean, seriously, going down the mine? Being a miner was a filthy, horrible job. Working in the semi-darkness for a whole shift, operating deafeningly loud machinery, shovelling huge amounts of coal into trucks, inhaling coal dust for eight hours or more, and don't even ask about toilet facilities –there weren't any!

I leave the implications of that to your imagination.

As for working on the farms, I had already done my share of this. I did some part-time work in the fields locally to supplement my very meagre pocket money. I remember one job in particular. I was picking fruit. I don't know if you know, but gooseberries grow on low bushes, and the branches are exceedingly prickly, with long, tough thorns. It was back-breaking work, and the thorns ripped and tore at my hands, even strong gloves didn't help that much. By the end of the day I was bleeding, exhausted and very, very sore. Then I had to come back again the next day and repeat the whole experience!

On another job I drove the tractor for potato picking. Less backbreaking, so you would think it was a better job, but it was no less exhausting, and hugely boring at the same time. It involved driving a tractor very slowly – literally at one or two miles an hour – up and down an enormous field. It was hypnotically monotonous.

The tractor pulled a cart. Into this cart the potato picking machine would pour its harvest. You couldn't doze off because you had to keep the tractor precisely in the right position. You had to pull forward or back from time to time to keep the cartload of potatoes evenly spread. Too far and you lost some of the precious crop. Did I mention you were almost shaken to pieces? You also got covered in dust and soil.

When I lay in bed at the end of a long day of potato

picking, I had the strangest sensation. It was as if the whole world was going backwards at two miles an hour! It made me feel sick.

Well, anyway, you can see why I was desperate to escape the village and find a career that *didn't* involve back-breaking, filthy work in the mine or on the farm.

The avenue I lived in consisted of council houses. They were well-built, three-bedroomed, red-brick 1950s semis, with a good amount of garden, at a rent working people could afford. Many people spent their whole lives in these houses. They were a heck of a lot better than the coal-board houses, hastily erected down the road in the previous five years or so. The new houses were built to accommodate the miners and their families from Derbyshire, where the pits had closed because, it was said, they had become 'uneconomical'. These houses were pokey, and not nearly so well built.

Within a very few years all the coal mines in Britain would be closed, including Dad's, but luckily he had retired by then. In 1967, however, my father worked, above ground, at the pit. He was responsible for the machinery that operated the 'cage' – the lift that took the miners down to the coal face. This meant he was also responsible for checking the men for matches and cigarettes. Mines and flames are not a good mix! For much of the shift he was able to sit and read.

My mother worked at Woolworths in the local market town. Both of my parents were as ambitious for me as I was for myself. They wanted me to do well at school, and thus escape the lowly paid occupations on offer locally.

My father had no real understanding of what a university education meant. The careers he had in mind for me involved apprenticeships, training courses. Careers like plumbing, carpentry, practical work like that. Perhaps being the boss of my own firm eventually. It all sounded a bit too much like hard work to me!

Dad thought this way because he himself was very good with his hands. He mended clocks, he did all the maintenance on the house and on the car. He would have loved for me to follow in his footsteps (or should that be handprints?). To his great disappointment, when it came to anything practical, I was utterly useless!

I managed to break stuff, make a mess of things, or of myself, every time I tried to help with decorating, do-it-yourself, or maintaining the car. In the end, he gave up on me.

Academically, on the other hand, I was more of a success. I had passed the eleven-plus exam, and I was now doing my 'A' levels at the grammar school in Westford near where my mother worked. It was a school with a proud history of students going on to Oxford and Cambridge; it even grudgingly acknowledged that there were other universities. I was determined: *I* was going to go to university. It didn't matter which, anything to get out of Dokesley. I had every confidence I would get there – despite my congenital laziness when it came to such mundane tasks as essay writing and exam revision!

As for my social life, well, what social life? I was a very lonely teenager. I had no girlfriend, I was very shy with girls. I attended a boys' school, so I really didn't come across girls socially very much. They were a complete mystery to me, a different species as far as I was concerned.

But then I was a social misfit with other boys too. My few male friends tended to be oddballs and loners like myself. We gravitated together. I had suffered a great deal of bullying in my younger schooldays, less so at the moment, but there were still times when the village bullies thought I was fair game. Like in the café at Westford that day.

I was socially inept, and clumsy, in every sense. Looking back, I can put it down to an undiagnosed dyspraxia, which no one at the time had even heard of. It affects the way your brain co-ordinates with your body. As far as parents and teachers were concerned, I was just a 'clumsy child'. I was the last one in the whole of my primary school to learn how to tie my school tie and my shoelaces, my writing was a complete mess, and I was hopeless at ball games. In addition, I was not particularly articulate… in fact, it would have been impossible for me to say, 'particularly articulate!'

No one expected great things from me. The surprise when I passed the eleven-plus was gratifying and insulting at the same time! Added to this, I was shy and skinny, as well as stutteringly incoherent. So, it's no surprise, that at the age of seventeen, I had no girlfriend!

Our back garden looked out onto arable land, fields. Fields that were just now full of cabbage-like kale plants and yellow rapeseed – cattle food for the dairy farms round. Further in the distance, from my bedroom window Dokesley woods could be seen, a local beauty spot.

In between the fields and the woods, there were the remnants of buildings left over from the Second World War. There were two whole sets of air raid shelters, for example. We used to play in them when I was younger. It was beyond me at the time why anyone thought that the Germans would want to bomb this miserable place!

There was also a little hamlet of six large Nissen huts. These were buildings which could be put up quickly, in an emergency such as flooding or war. In these huts, around thirty refugees had been housed after being displaced by the war. Dokesley's refugees were Polish, mainly. They had moved on some years before, most of them back home to Poland. By 1967 the little temporary hamlet was long abandoned, and the huts were rotting away. They were an eyesore in the countryside, with weeds breaking through the concrete road, and brown rust discolouring the 'stainless' steel semi-circular buildings.

I envisaged long days and weeks doing very little

during the summer holidays. I anticipated kicking about the village, maybe going swimming in the swimming pool in Westford, or sitting at home in the garden, reading – I did a lot of reading – or playing cards with my best friend, Tom.

— CHAPTER TWO —

The Stone Drops

This was the situation then, on that warm, wet July night, as I slept peacefully in my bed in the back bedroom of the house. I had sensitive hearing which made me a light sleeper. I couldn't get to sleep if there was any noise – any noise at all. I even wrapped the clock in one of my shirts and pushed it into a drawer, because its tick kept me awake.

That night, my hair-trigger hearing detected an alien sound. It was the sound of someone climbing stealthily down from the windowsill, onto the floor, near the foot of my bed. The floor creaked, very slightly. I was awake immediately, though still dozy and sleep drugged. I froze. The hairs on the back of my neck stood up. I could hear someone breathing. I lay stock still, while I considered what to do. Should I confront the intruder? Or should I shout for help? That was more like it. I was basically a coward at heart.

I dithered, unsure of which course to take. In the end I took neither. I lay still while I tried to wake up enough to make up my mind. I opened half an eye, discreetly. Dim light filtered in though the closed curtains – enough to see a little. The breather was outlined in profile against the window. So, I hadn't dreamt it! There *was* someone in my bedroom! I don't know why I didn't challenge them, or at least shout for help, but I didn't. Perhaps it was because the figure was very clearly that of a female.

Hardly daring to breathe, I reached out and I turned on the lamp by my bed and I stared at the figure in front of me, who had frozen into statue-like immobility at my first movement.

It was indeed a girl, one of about my own age. Her trim figure was dressed in black. She had got wet in the rain – it was pouring by now. Her wet clothes clung to her; rather fetchingly, I thought. She had a pretty face with a turned-up nose. Sarah Miles, the actress had just been in *Those Magnificent Men in Their Flying Machines*. I saw it at the Westford cinema. I really fancied her. This girl's nose was like Sarah's.

In the light of the bedside lamp, I couldn't help noticing she had a rather pretty mouth, too, with full red lips. Currently her lips were parted in shock. Time came to a complete halt, as I gawped at this apparition, and she gawped at me.

Now I could see her clearly, I could see she had green eyes and flame-red hair tied up neatly in a bun. All in all, she looked, to me, like an angel. There was an angel in my bedroom! Maybe I *was* still dreaming.

Or was my fantasy life invading my reality?

I don't know who was more startled. If I'd had any idea of shouting for help, it had gone. I just gaped, like someone in a trance.

The pretty mouth issued an ugly word; one that my parents would not have approved of! So much for being an angel! 'Please don't cry out. I'm not here to hurt you, or to steal anything. They're after me and I need a place to hide.'

I opened and shut my mouth a few times. I couldn't think of a single thing to say. All my awkwardness with girls rose up and choked off speech. I felt hot and knew I must be blushing bright red. Damn!

There was a girl in my room! An actual girl in my actual bedroom! She padded over to me. Like a cat, she moved silently and elegantly. I gulped. I had rarely been so close to a girl. I had certainly never had one in my bedroom before. I could have reached out and touched her face. I could smell her. Her aroma was a mix of perfume, sweat and rain-dampened clothes. I clung to the bedclothes, protecting my modesty. My head spun with her closeness. At that crucial moment, before either of us could speak further, there came a loud knock at the front door downstairs. The spell was broken. She looked towards the sound. She became urgent. She turned those huge green eyes on me.

'Hide me! Please?' I gaped on like some kind of idiot. Then, more peremptorily, 'Please!'

That was when I told her to get under the bed. It

then occurred to me that if I closed the windows, it would cover up the fact that someone had got in that way. So, I did. I moved like someone in a trance, or a dream, without speaking.

I switched out the light and lay back down. Just in time. There came a second knock downstairs. I heard my father switch on the light in the bedroom he shared with my mother. There was a pause for a few moments while he put on his dressing gown, then I heard him open the door, emerge from the room, cross the landing and make his ponderous way downstairs.

I heard voices in the hall: my father, who was a bit cross at being woken up, and another man, being conciliatory. I couldn't make out everything they were saying, but I caught a few words.

'Police… searching… criminal.'

After a minute or two my father's heavy tread came back up the stairs. There was a knock on my door, and he opened it.

I made the pretence of waking up and reaching for the lamp. 'W-What's happening, D-Dad?' I asked, innocently.

'It's the police, they're looking for someone. They want to look around our garden.'

'Oh, OK. If that's all it is, I'll tell the g-girls to come out from under the b-bed then!'

'You and your jokes! Go back to sleep, you idiot.' But he said it affectionately. At least, I think he did…

'Night, D-Dad.'

'Night.'

He made his way back downstairs, to keep an eye on the police, as they searched our back garden for the miscreant. Finally, I heard the men come back into the house, and then leave. I was imagining all sorts of scenarios. I had read a good many books. One of my favourite series was the stories about Raffles. Was this the female equivalent of that famous gentleman jewel thief?

There was silence for a little time, then a whisper from under the bed, 'I'm coming out!'

She slid silently out. I gazed at her shadowy form in the darkness, still hypnotised by the situation. I switched on the lamp, to see her better. I at least expected some sort of thank you. She shattered the moment.

'You idiot!' She hissed in a forceful whisper. 'I nearly sh… nearly had a heart attack when you said that about someone under the bed!'

'I thought that was a good b-bluff!' I replied indignantly. 'Dad knows me. He knows I've never had one g-girl in my bedroom! Let alone *girls* p-plural… Anyway, the police are looking for you. You're a c-criminal. You're lucky I didn't g-give you up.'

'All right, all right! Thank you, I'm sure.' I'd never heard such a sarcastic thank you in my life! She followed it with, 'Don't you ever dust under there? Look at me!' She was now covered in dust and fluff, which clung enthusiastically to her wet clothes. She looked a sight. I didn't care. Even with smuts on her nose and cheeks, and dust all over clothes, she still looked great to me! I gazed admiringly.

This was turning out to be just about the longest conversation I'd ever had with a girl. I was about to say something to spoil the whole thing.

'Anyone ever t-told you how p-pretty you are?'

'Oh God. Really? Is that the best you can do? Yes, my dad, all the time, and he was a twit too! Just when I was starting to like you a little bit. Listen, don't get any ideas. I know I'm in your bedroom, but I'm not getting in that bed with you, so don't even think about it!'

I hadn't. It was at that moment I realised something. It was unusual for me to have a conversation with someone my own age, who didn't mock my stammer – or at least comment on it. She rose several points further in my estimation.

Just then Dad's footstep sounded on the stairs. He had said goodbye to the 'police' and was coming back to bed. With a gasp, forgetting everything she had just said, she dived under the covers beside me. I turned out my light. She stayed there, lying close to me, hidden by the heap of blankets and eiderdown. Dad made his way to the bathroom, and then went back to bed again. Luckily, this time, he didn't come in.

When he had turned the light out and got back into bed, she flung back the covers and sat up, panting like someone who had been underwater. I had a grin big enough to split my face; I couldn't help it.

'Don't you dare say *anything!*' she hissed. 'That was not fun, believe me. Haven't you heard of bloody deodorant? And you wear pyjamas to bed? In the summer?'

I'd had just about enough. All my cherished ideas of what girls should be like, were being completely shattered in one brief encounter! Women were supposed to be modest, shy, well-spoken and well, feminine – 'sugar and spice and all things nice'. Not foul-mouthed criminals. Especially not criminals who insult the people that help them. Talk about biting the hand that feeds you!

Have you ever had an argument in whispers? It's really, really difficult! But we did our best, hissing at each other like leaky steam engines.

'I've never m-met anyone like you! You swear, you insult me, when I'm only trying to help you out! And look, you've made my b-bed wet!'

'A change from you doing it I suppose!' she retorted. I was too taken aback at this to reply. My mouth just hung open. See, not particularly articulate! She continued, 'Look, you, you male chauvinist. I am *not* a damsel in distress, I can take care of myself!' I shook my head to recover from this tirade. My blood was up now.

'Really?' I hissed 'Then why don't I call the police and hand you over?' That was a bluff, of course. We didn't have a phone. There was the telephone box up the road, and one of our neighbours a few houses away, had a phone. That was the sum total for the whole village. Besides there was no way I was actually going to give her away. I didn't care what she had done; I didn't even care how she spoke to me. I had never met such an incredible girl... I wanted to, was desperate to, get to know her better.

'I can see I'll have to tell you some things, secret things. You really can't tell anyone else, ever. Not your family, not your girlfriend, not your friends, no one. Understand, bonehead?'

'A-All right, a-all *right!* I g-get it, OK? I'm *not* a bonehead... And I d-don't have a girlfriend.' I added sulkily.

'Well, there's a surprise! OK. Listen...' She sat on my bed and proceeded to tell me the most unlikely story I had ever heard. But I listened all right. How could I not? She fascinated me... anyway her mouth was so attractive when she spoke – when she wasn't swearing or insulting me, that is.

— CHAPTER THREE —
The Ripples Begin to Spread

She was training to be a spy, she told me. There was a top secret government project to train teenagers as secret agents. Posing as children/young people, they were less likely to be suspected – so the theory went.

It was the end of her year-long training and she was performing one final test. A real mission. Her class of five trainees had been delegated one task each, under the supervision of a qualified agent. They were scattered all over the country. The jobs were relatively minor in importance, but genuine spy-type work all the same. Missions that should not be too dangerous, and where it wouldn't matter, too much, if they failed. She made it clear that she had no intention of failing!

Her mission was to go to those Nissen huts just outside the village, to try and locate a code-breaking machine. The story went like this:

In the late fifties, some of the Polish refugees had been visited by other Polish people. Ostensibly these were relatives coming over for a visit from Poland. In fact, they were people connected with the communist government. It was the height of the cold war. The newcomers had brought a coding machine. The idea was to set up a cell of Polish communist sympathisers in this country. This secret coder was one of a number brought over so that the communist cells in Britain could communicate with each other by radio.

Apparently the British authorities had somehow discovered this plot – the girl guessed that one of the Dokesley Poles gave the game away. Special Branch raided the place and carted everyone off. That explained all the stories locally, about the fact that the refugees all disappeared really suddenly. It had happened some years before, when I was small. They had gone so quickly in fact, that it caused comment in the village. They were there one day, gone the next. Now I knew why! After a while the gossip died down and people forgot the Poles and got on with their lives.

Somehow the British spy authorities had found out that one of the coding machines had been inadvertently left behind when the Polish people were rounded up, some ten years before. The machine was more precious than gold. It would help MI5 to decode secret transmissions sent to and from the communist government in Poland; Poland being, at that time, a puppet state of the Soviet Union, bitter enemy of the western powers, which included Britain.

'It should have been easy,' she complained bitterly, 'I was told it would be a piece of cake. I was also told there were no enemy agents in this area. All I had to do was find this bleedin' thing and bring it back. I was given a week to complete the mission.' She stopped and shook her head in frustration. She bit her bottom lip.

She had my rapt attention. If she was making it up, it was an amazing piece of invention!

'W-what happened? What went wrong?' I asked.

'Enemy agents were there, waiting for me. I barely got into the access road before they jumped me. I had the shock of my life. The first guy grabbed me by my coat, but I managed to shake him off, and I ran, leaving him holding the jacket. A pity, I really liked that coat! They were blocking my path back to my car, I couldn't escape that way, so I just turned and ran in the opposite direction. I ran and ran, towards these houses. I managed to lose them on the edge of the village. I saw your window open and made a beeline for it.'

'Don't you have a g-gun?'

'Are you stupid? No, I don't have a gun! You think they give teenage trainees guns? I shouldn't have needed a gun, there should have been no opposition!'

'Shh!'

'Sorry! But you are such a twit!'

'Thanks a lot! Er, what will you do now?' I was sort of hoping she might say 'stay here for a bit', but she didn't.

Her jaw tightened and she stuck out her chin. 'I have to go back. I have a mission to finish.' There was a phrase at the time, applied to test pilots and astronauts. It was said they had the 'right stuff'. I thought that here was someone who had 'the right stuff' all right! My admiration was growing. Personally, though, I thought she was crackers to even think of going back out there!

'But won't they catch you again? They might hurt you, or-or kill you.'

She gave me a look I didn't understand. Then, a bit more gently she whispered, 'I have to risk it.' Her lower lip trembled, it was the first sign I'd seen of any kind of weakness. My heart lurched. I think that's when I really started to fall for her. 'I must, don't you see? I have to, to complete my training. I really need to do this, I…' She was forgetting to whisper in her vehemence.

'Sshh! OK, OK. You have to do it.' I took a deep breath. Then I heard someone say something.

'I'll come with you.' I heard the words very clearly. It was a full five seconds before I realised that I was the one who had said it! I'll never know to this day what made me do it. It was like hearing someone else speaking, but no it was me: lazy, comfortable, cowardly me!

It's hard to emphasise exactly just how much scornful contempt she could put into one word.

'YOU?!'

She had to put her hand over her mouth to prevent her derisive laughter from echoing around the house.

'Yes, *me*! And there's no need to be like that.' I was genuinely hurt. My confidence, never great, was torn to shreds.

'Look. There's nothing that says I have to help you… I'm still not sure I shouldn't hand you over to the police!' I paused to calm down a bit. I breathed heavily for a moment, then I went on, 'Listen to me. I know a back way into those huts. I can get you there without going onto the road. Anyway, if you're looking for something, it'll be quicker with two of us.'

There was that appraising look again. It was as if I was a specimen in a laboratory; one which had just done something interesting, something against all expectations!

'Listen, you're a nice guy, you really are. I mean, thanks and all that, but it's really not safe. *I* don't have a gun, but *they* will have. I can't have you to worry about, you'd be a millstone round my neck.'

Now my hackles were really up. She was maddening! I had gathered up all my courage to offer her help, and she was throwing it back in my face. Damn her insufferable pride!

'I am *not* a millstone! It's dangerous for you too!' I paused to get my breath and to calm down a bit. 'Look. I'll keep out of your way, I promise. I can keep watch while you look for this, this thing…What does it look like anyway?' It was during this little speech that I realised that I actually hadn't stammered for quite a while.

I thought she was going to refuse again, or say something sarcastic, but she seemed taken aback. 'Oh, er, it's a bit like a sort of electric typewriter device. There's more to it than that, but that's what it looks like, in a kind of metal case.'

'OK, then. Let's go.'

'You're not only an idiot, you're a fool as well...but I'll say this, you've got guts! All right, if you're determined to come, be it on your own head!'

'Great!'And I meant it! She hated me. She thought I was an idiot, but I didn't care. She was letting me go with her! I was going to spend more time with this rude, insulting, maddening, brave, smashing girl. Progress!

CHAPTER FOUR

Plunging into the Water

I got out of bed to get dressed, self-conscious and red-faced. I was very aware of her sardonic gaze, and her sarcastic comments about my pyjamas. I couldn't take them off, not with her watching! So, I pulled my clothes on over the top of them. Once dressed, I reached for my nice warm rainproof parka coat, got it from the wardrobe and started to put it on. As I was tugging the first sleeve over my arm, bulked up by pyjama and jumper sleeves, I looked at her. The enemy spies took her jacket, when they tried to grab her. She looked wet and cold. I paused. I pulled the parka off. Reluctantly, I handed it over.

'You have it,' I remarked, rather generously, I thought! 'It will keep you warm and dry.'

It was my pride and joy, that coat. It was full-length, in dull green and it had a hood with fake fur trim. They were all the rage back then. It was the badge of the mods. You were either a mod or a rocker, depending on whether you preferred soul, rhythm-

and-blues and ska (mods) or Elvis (rockers). I sort of preferred Bach and Beethoven, but I kept that quiet.

'Well, OK. Thanks!' She was not tall, and the parka rather swamped her, but the night was turning wet and chilly. The Parka was warm and cosy; and it would keep off the worst of the rain. 'I would never have guessed you were a mod!' she exclaimed as she hugged the coat around herself.

I gave her a weak smile. I wore a black t-shirt, my black school trousers and my dark blue gabardine school mac, with the collar turned up. I felt like a real spy! Shame I didn't have a proper spy hat. I only had a bright yellow bobble hat, knitted by my mum; somehow it wasn't the right image! I left it behind.

I put on my cross-country running shoes, which had rippled soles, for better grip on muddy surfaces. They were nothing like the cross-country studs of today, but over muddy courses they were better than nothing. I had no other shoes but my boring black school shoes. They would be no good in the muddy fields, besides which it would ruin them. Nobody wore trainers in those days, there were no such thing! P.E. at school was done in black canvas shoes called plimsoles.

Before we left, I opened my bedroom window again, so that it would be nice and cool and fresh when I got back. Sleep was important to me, and I couldn't sleep in an over-warm room – always supposing I got back!

We crept out of the house, through the back door and into the garden. The night was now distinctly chillier as we slipped along the garden path between the rows of runner beans and peas, past the compost heap and down to the chain-link fence at the bottom of the back garden. We climbed over the fence into the field behind our house. We crouched down for a moment among the wet foliage, as our eyes adjusted to the darkness.

'What's that smell?' she hissed, 'It's foul.'

'It's kale,' was my reply, 'It smells worse because it's wet.'

'Oh God, I hate the country!'

'Come on, there's a track down here.' There was a diagonal path through the kale, invisible from outside the field. You had to know it was there. I took it and she followed. Not only was it still raining, but we were crawling through the soaking wet plants on our hands and knees, getting muddier and wetter with every movement.

'Oh god, I hate the flippin' country!' she repeated. 'This is bloody horrible!' I didn't reply. What could I say? It was. But at least we couldn't be seen by anyone watching the roads.

The rapeseed field was better. It was surrounded by a tall hedge, which concealed us from the road. I led us around the edge, away from the wet foliage and on down the hill. I was coated with cold, clammy mud. The water seeped through my school trousers and my pyjama trousers, making them cling uncomfortably to my legs as we went. At the bottom of the field, we pushed our way through a hole in the hedge. We emerged into the back of the Nissen hut 'hamlet.'

'OK, I'll give that to you. Good navigating!' she whispered in my ear as she tried to squeeze the water out of the bottom of her trousers. 'My shoes will never be the same, though!'

We paused for a moment and looked towards the little collection of temporary housing. There were six large huts, in various degrees of disrepair. Each hut was made in a semi-circular design, like a massive baked bean can, stripped of its label and lying on its side, half-buried in the ground.

Even in the daytime this wasn't an attractive place. At night it was positively eerie; throw in sinister shadows and feelings of foreboding, and you can see why my heart was in my mouth.

More than thirty people had been housed here during the war and through into the 1950s, in this very basic accommodation. The place had been completely deserted for some years. The huts were not luxurious places to live, but they could be put up quickly – and cheaply. They made a decent temporary refuge for people who had fled the Nazis, with nothing but the clothes on their backs.

I knew those huts. I had played there. In daylight they still bore signs of their previous occupation. By day, a can of Vim (a kitchen cleaner) could be seen in one window, a lone curtain hung mournfully in another. There were pans and kettles, and other detritus, all left behind in the sudden enforced flit – pathetic little reminders of the people who had sought refuge here from the Nazis, only to go home and find the communists were almost as bad!

The huts lay there, abandoned, rusting away quietly. That was another thing, the eerie silence. There was not a sound apart from the incessant rain. The noise of it blocked the ears, the darkness blinded the eyes. It was like feeling your way through the velvet night blindfolded and with earplugs in. It was hard enough to see a hand in front of your face.

We crept up to the nearest hut and peeped round the corner. I winced as freezing cold water trickled down my neck, dripping from the overhanging roof. From here we could see the concrete access road, a faint grey stain in the stygian gloom. It ran down past the huts so that vehicles could come into the stainless-steel hamlet.

The girl nudged me and pointed. I strained my eyes. Through the rain and darkness I finally managed to make out what she was pointing at. She had sharp eyes. There was a man. He was just barely visible. He was on sentry duty, some fifty yards away, on the roadway. He was standing at the junction with the lane that led down from Dokesley. His two colleagues were probably still searching the houses in the village, under the guise of British police officers. He had been stationed there, in case his quarry doubled back from Dokesley. In the other direction, the lane eventually wound on towards the main A1 trunk road, a mile away.

His quarry was crouching next to me. She swore again.

'They've left a sentry in case I came back. Hell. Now what do we do?'

I suddenly felt an irresistible urge to do something; to show this amazing girl that I could play a part in her mission. I thought for a few moments. I had an inspiration. It was, of course, based on things I had seen on the telly and in films. There was not a lot to do in Dokesley, other than watch television. Even then there were only three channels, and our set was black and white. We didn't get a colour telly until later that year.

'Leave him to me,' said a voice,' you just find that machine.' It sounded very fine. I just wished it hadn't been me that had said it! By the Lord Harry, I'd done it again! There was no going back now!

'If they haven't already found it…Wait, why what are you going to do?'

Why on earth was I getting involved? What the heck was I doing here in the cold wet night? I mean for goodness sake; I was scared of my own shadow! I hated confrontation of any kind, which had made life easy for the bullies! But now, in front of this fabulous girl, I had spoken up and I couldn't back down.

Afterwards I had nightmares for days!

I was a great fan of adventure programmes like *The Saint*. I remembered the kind of tricks Simon Templar got up to on the telly. I decided to try one.

'Never you mind,' I heard myself say,' Just get that, that typewriter thing. They haven't found it, or else why would they still be here? They're probably going to come back in daylight to search properly for it.' I started forward, then I felt a restraining hand on my arm. She leaned in and gave me a kiss on the cheek.

'Take care of yourself!' She breathed in my ear.

I set off into the night. After that kiss – and her warm breath on my ear – I was tingling all over and floating on air!

As I ran, reality came back with a crash.

Oh well, that's the end of that! I thought, as I ran. *I guess I'll never see her again.*

You know, I'm not one to boast. I'm all too aware of my weaknesses. As I've said, I was useless at sport. Anything involving a ball and I was lost. Put a racquet in my hand and be prepared to duck! But there was one thing I *could* do. I could run like the wind. I was captain of the school cross country team. In a boys' school you had to be good at sport. Running had saved my psyche.

The man on sentry-go was looking up and down the road that led back to the village. He wore the obligatory raincoat, fastened up tight against the rain, with the collar up, and a hat – everyone wore hats in those days. He walked backwards and forwards a bit, flapping his arms to keep warm. I watched from my hiding place as he took out a cigarette from a packet in his pocket and tried to light it while shielding it from the rain. While he was preoccupied with this, I crept up behind the hedge that lined the lane to Dokesley. I got as close to him as I could get without being seen. My poor shirt and trousers would never be the same again after this night's work, but at least I was hard to see in the gloom, dressed in dark clothes and mud! To add to the camouflage, I smeared my muddy hands all over my face.

I was counting on the fact that, in the dark, one running black-clothed figure would be hard to distinguish from another, even one of the wrong sex. From my position crouched down behind the hedge, while he was lighting his cigarette, I picked up a pebble and threw it. (If it was good enough for Simon Templar, it was good enough for me!)

It whizzed down the road to my right, towards the village. It landed with a clatter. The man's head shot round as if it were on a spring, he peered short-sightedly into the night. His hand went to his pocket, and he ran off along the road back towards the houses of Dokesley.

I couldn't believe it actually worked! I stood up from my hiding place and crept along the hedge to the access road. I emerged from the Nissen hut estate and stood at the junction. I waited just long enough for him to turn and see me. There were no streetlights. There were no streetlights anywhere in Dokesley. That's the kind of out of the way place it was. Streetlights didn't come to the village until two years later; and this was a country road, little more than a lane, with no lights anywhere near. All he could possibly have seen from thirty yards away, was a shadow in the dark night. He caught sight of me as I waited at the junction of the access road with the lane, a black figure against the white concrete road.

I heard him shout: '*остановитьили я стрелять*!' It sounded like '*ostanavit il y a strelyat*'. I guessed he was telling me to stop.

He's got to be kidding! I thought and set off at a sprint down the lane, away from the Nissen huts, away from the village and towards the woods. I heard his footsteps on the concrete roadway, as he pounded along after me. I climbed a gate on the left of the road and cut across the field. This was cross country all right! I was in my element. I think I actually laughed. Then I heard a gunshot. He was firing his gun! The man was actually shooting at me! The laughter died on my lips. I ran faster, terrified, heart pounding fit to burst its way out of my chest. I was convinced that any moment I would be shot. He didn't fire again though – either because it was too dark to see or because it was too difficult to aim while running.

I squelched downhill through the muddy field, picking up at least two pounds of mud on each foot, heading towards a bridge across a nearby stream. The stream marked the boundary of Dokesley woods. I paused on the bridge to catch my breath, and to scrape some of the mud off my shoes. He was trying to follow, but he was struggling in the clinging clay soil. He didn't have ripples on his shoes like I did. I didn't want him to give up and go back to the huts, so I let him catch up a little way and then I was off again. I crossed the bridge and turned left, running along the path beside the river. Once again, I outpaced him.

Further on, the river took a bend to the right, flowing away from Dokesley village, which was now on my left. There was a tree across the stream at this point. I had played all around here my whole life, and the tree had been there for as long as I could remember. It was crossable with care, but there was a trick to it. It rolled when you got halfway, if you were not careful, and pitched you into the water. I knew that from personal experience, and I knew the trick. The stranger following me, of course, had no idea!

I skipped along the fallen tree, over the waters running below. I paused on the other side as if I was puffed, but really to see what would happen. Sure enough, he followed me. He was overweight and clearly no gymnast! He had to put his gun away in order to use both hands to steady himself, as he negotiated the tree trunk across the stream; with its branches sticking out at all angles. He took the crossing carefully and slowly. It made no difference. Good old tree! It turned and threw him into the water with a satisfying SPLOSH! After a wet couple of weeks, the river was swollen; it was about four feet deep. He was swept off his feet, and carried along by the current, floundering around. He wasn't going to be chasing anyone for some time!

I made sure he saw me heading in the vague direction of Dokesley, away from the Nissen huts and the girl. I put on my best burst of speed, leaving him flailing around in the chest-deep water, being swept downstream. I went home by a circuitous route. There was noone to be seen as I trotted up Whitely Avenue – my avenue –and slipped round to the back of my house, number twenty-six. I climbed up onto the brick-built shed/coal-house – a feature of the council houses –and from there I managed to reach my own bedroom window. Thank goodness I had left it open! I climbed back in with a hearty sigh of relief and sat for a good few minutes on the bed, shaking all over.

When my legs would support me again, I stood up and undressed. I gratefully stripped off all my clothes, including my pyjamas. I was soaked right through to the skin. The girl would be too, after that trip across the kale field, and the rain. As for the man left on sentry duty. Well, after his dip in the river he would be wetter than the two of us put together!

I sneaked silently into the bathroom and washed as much of me as I could, as quietly as I could. I towelled myself down. I even tried to wash the crosscountry shoes in the bath. It was not a great success. I then had to clean the bath. I fell back into bed over an hour after I got back.

What a start to the summer holidays! Only now, when it was over, did it really come home to me what I had just done. I had allowed myself to be chased, for two miles across the countryside, by a man with a gun. A real gun, for goodness sake, with real bullets! I don't know what my parents would have said, but it would have been something forceful. The word idiot would have figured greatly! I decided not to tell them about it.

I had a chilling flashback of him firing the gun. The bang rolled around in my memory like continuous thunder. I started shaking then, and I continued shaking on and off for three whole days! At least I knew now that she was telling the truth. She really was a teenage spy, and she really had been in considerable danger... and I had helped her! Me!

I lay there in bed, my heart rate slowly coming back to something like normal. I began to get drowsy. Before I nodded off, it occurred to me that my Parka was gone for good. How was I going to explain that to my parents? As it was, I was going to have to clean the bedroom floor and wash all my clothes discreetly while they were out at work. How did that washing machine work?

Oh well, I had exchanged a coat for an adventure. As my eyes were closing, I thought about the girl. It was worth it. *She* was worth it. I had never met anyone like her in my life. I didn't know girls like that existed.

What a girl! Pity I didn't get her name, I thought as I drifted off. *James Bond would certainly have done better! He would have got her name, telephone number and at least a kiss on the lips!*

I sighed, turned over in bed and fell into a deep sleep, exhausted from the running, but also from the excitement. No clock would have woken me that night. Not even an Acme four bells alarm clock, as seen in all the best cartoons!

I didn't wake again until well after my parents had got up and gone to work. When I came to, sometime around eleven o'clock the next morning, I thought that the whole thing must have been a crazy dream. Then I saw my wet, muddy clothes on the floor, and I knew it had been real after all. And that was not all I saw. There, hanging up behind the bedroom door was my Parka! How? She must have come back in the night, and this time had made sure to avoid the creaking floorboard! I threw off the bedclothes and staggered awkwardly out of bed. My legs were stiff and aching from the run. I hobbled to the door, picked up my Parka and smelled it. Behind the smell of mud and Kale – and stale me –there was the delectable trace of her scent. There was something in the pocket. A note:

Country boy,
I found it! It was hidden under the floor in one of the

huts. I never saw the man again. I see you got home safely.
Thanks, mate.
Elise.

'It' obviously referred to the coding machine. *Well done, Elise!* I thought. And, actually, *well done, me!*

— CHAPTER FIVE —
A Rolling Stone

After that excitement, life in the village seemed duller than ever. I was more restless and even more fed up with the place than usual. It wasn't just the adventure, contrasted with the ensuing boredom. It was *her*. I was sure I would never see her again; but I couldn't get her out of my mind – if that was where she was? Out of my heart? Soul? Some other part? I had read enough books to know that love could take you like this, but I thought they were exaggerating! It's like a fatal disease, somehow you think it's never going to happen to you! Had I really fallen in love in a couple of short hours with that amazing, infuriating girl?

I looked at myself in the mirror. Not a pretty sight. I looked away quickly! I addressed myself sternly.

'Be realistic,' I declared to the mirror. 'Why on earth should she fancy *you*? You need to forget her!'

Hah! That was easier said than done. I mean, I tried, I really did, but my mind/heart/soul/other bits, kept remembering her in spite of me. As the days went by that summer, I found my thoughts turning back to her, time and again. She had really got under my skin.

I spent a lot of that time with my best friend, Tom. He was a year older than me and had moved to the area a few years before with his family. They lived in the miners' housing up the road. The road he lived on was called Lakefield Avenue. The two roads joined on, end to end. It made one straight line, with the occasional little close to left and right. It was one long straight walk up to his and back to mine.

Tom had attended the local Secondary Modern school, which was where you went if you failed the eleven-plus. He hated it there. He left at sixteen, as soon as he could, and took an apprenticeship with a local engineering firm. Like me, he had a bent for the gentler things in life: art for example and reading – although I could never appreciate his taste in music. He enjoyed a mixture of soul, Motown and the plain weird. Yoko Ono singing 'Open your Box', and someone calling himself Napoleon XIV singing 'They're Coming to Take Me Away, Ha-Haaa!'. (Nowadays you can look these up on YouTube, but you'll wish you hadn't!)

We played cards, not for money, for neither of us had any! And we talked, and we talked: about all sorts of things. Life, generally; our lives in particular. Mainly we talked about how we couldn't wait to leave Dokesley. We were desperate to get out of the place. We both had a yen to get to London. Secretly now though, I just wanted to be wherever Elise was!

Patience was not a major facet of Tom's personality. We were playing cards one night, a week or so after my adventure with Elise. I was thinking about her instead of about the game. I was distracted, miles away. I was staring unseeing at the cards through my reading glasses. He told me off.

'I like winning, mantod,' – he called me mantod for some reason he never really explained – 'but I like a *bit* of competition! Come on, make a game of it!' He sighed.

I had to explain my distracted behaviour. I was bursting to talk about it anyway. It was torture not to be able to speak of her to somebody, anybody. I couldn't tell him everything, because I had promised her. I told him I had met a girl. I told him about her sarcasm, her swearing, and her pretty face.

He was not especially sympathetic. To be fair, Tom had problems of his own. Recently, he had admitted to me that he was gay, although we didn't use that meaning of the word in those days. I had no idea. That's how naïve I was. Apparently, my parents had guessed. Unbeknownst to me they were getting a bit concerned with me hanging out with him. I just thought it was, well, Tom. He was a unique individual in all sorts of ways, quite eccentric. It made no real difference to our friendship; in fact it made it a bit more open. Now he could speak about things he hadn't been able to speak about before.

We didn't go to the same school, but we had gravitated together in the village because we suffered a similar problem – being different. His parents were neither patient nor tolerant. So, he hadn't told them he was gay. He hadn't 'come out' to them. In the end he never did come out to them. If they hadn't worked it out for themselves, they never knew.

His 'father' was actually his stepfather. After Tom's real father died, his mother married again. This new man was a rough tough Welsh miner, younger than his wife, and steeped in working class values, like the rest of Dokesley. He didn't take to Tom at all. In his eyes art, theatre, music – brass bands excepted – and any hint of an interest in the finer things of life, was 'soppy'. He had no time for 'soppiness'. Anyone of a sensitive nature was a 'sissy'. Tom hated him and he used to come around to our house at every opportunity to get away from the toxic atmosphere at home.

Tom was always very thin, and one day, years later, he told me why. Apart from general neglect – which at least made him independent and self-reliant from an early age – his mother used to forget to feed him. It was as if she had forgotten that he was there!

This explained why Tom always seemed to arrive at our house around mealtimes! He knew he was likely to be invited in to share the meal.

Unsurprisingly, this led to a lifelong interest in food. In the next few years, he saved up his money, left home, went to London and trained to be a chef. He became very famous and wealthy, with a home in the famous Barbican complex in London, a villa in Spain and a *pied-à-terre* in Paris. Once he left Dokesley, he never looked back. But at this time, he was just my mate, the boy up the road, with an artistic soul; lost, adrift in this unsympathetic community, and broke, like me.

That night in early August, after we had finished playing cards at his house, I was making my way home. It was past ten at night. I looked down the street ahead of me and my heart sank. I could see two of the worst bullies of the village ahead of me, blocking my path. They were the ones who had seen me in the café in Westford.

They were fairly typical of the village youth. They were destined for dead-end jobs; they had no interest in anything but football; no pastimes more intellectual than walking down the back lane to the local pub. They shared Tom's dad's ideas about sensitivity and 'sissiness'. Ideas that were prevalent in the village as a whole.

I thought they looked like gorillas. It might have been my imagination, but it seemed to me that their knuckles may even have scraped along the ground as they walked. They were called Dennis Marks and Clive Dunthorpe. They left school at fifteen and went to work in the pit. They were the kind of youths who would have to think for a long time if you asked them difficult questions such as: 'What day is it today?'. They hadn't troubled me for a while now, but they had been spending their hard-earned pit money in the pub and on seeing me they decided to have some fun.

I sighed inwardly and swallowed hard. I prepared myself for the dreaded confrontation. They came forward, grinning. Suddenly, there she was. The girl, Elise. By my side. She had appeared out of nowhere. I didn't notice her until she was right next to me. I suppose they train spies to do that sort of thing, you know, generally sneaking up on people!

'Are they trouble?' she murmured in my ear.

I was concentrating on the two youths. I hadn't seen her. When she spoke, I jumped about two feet off the ground! After I had taken a second or two to recover from the shock, and my heart rate had slowed down to a manageable multiple of hundreds of beats per minute, I managed a reply.

'N-Not so much recently, but they used to g-give me a lot of trouble.'

She patted my arm and smiled. Then she turned and went right up to them. 'Evening boys!' she remarked. This threw the two boys rather. They were not quick thinkers, as I have mentioned. They needed time to absorb a new situation. They were certainly not used to attractive girls coming up voluntarily to speak to them. Elise was looking better than ever, she was wearing a cashmere coat, with a belt at her waist that tied rather than buckled. She looked wonderful.

They stood and stared at her, with their mouths agape.

'We're not going to have any trouble here, are we?' she asked, turning around so that she was standing between the two boys, facing me. She winked at me, unseen by them. Then she looked up at them in turn. She gently took one hand of each of them in hers and gave them a smile. They grinned, embarrassed. They had turned from predators to teddy bears. I wouldn't have been surprised if they had scraped their toes on the ground and said, 'Aw, shucks!'

She gracefully took a small step back, until she was slightly behind them, still holding their hands. She moved quickly, so quickly I couldn't follow what happened. In a trice she had the boy's arms so far up their backs that I could hear the creaking of shoulder joints.

'Are we, boys?'

They cried out in pain, then one of them managed to gasp, 'No, no trouble, aargh!'

'That's right. So why don't you go home and leave me and my boyfriend here to have a snog in peace. OK?' The creaking increased; so did the shouts of pain. 'I said, OK?'

'OK, OK!' they shouted.

'Oh, and just in case you might think of getting him on his own, later, I've taught him this trick!' With that she let them go. They ran for it. 'Night, boys!' she sang gaily.

'Wow, that was…'

She brushed herself down, straightened her coat, and interrupted me. 'Yes. Well don't get any ideas. Especially about snogging. I just said that to annoy them.'

'I don't care about the snogging, I'm just glad to see you again… Erm th-thanks for returning my coat.' Oh no, my stutter was back! 'A-and for s-saving me tonight.' I realised I was still wearing my reading glasses and whipped them off.

'One good turn deserves another.' She shrugged nonchalantly and smiled.

'B-but what are you d-doing here?'

'Are you stuttering?'

I nodded miserably. 'I always stutter when I'm talking to a g-girl,' I agonised, 'or if I'm n-nervous for some other r-reason.'

'You didn't stutter the other day.'

'I think you made me cross, you know, w-with all the s-sarcasm, and everything.'

'Obviously I shall have to keep being sarcastic.'

Silence.

'You avoided the c-creaky floorboard,' I declared, just for the sake of something to say. Mentally, I was desperately trying to summon up memories of angry feelings, in the hope of controlling my stammer. It wasn't working. I was being overwhelmed by feelings very different to anger. I went weak at the knees just standing next to her. 'You know? When you came back to return my c-coat?'

She looked at me.

'Oh, yeah. Well, never make the same mistake twice, that's part of our training. It was easy enough. Anyway, you were snoring like a pig. You wouldn't have heard a regiment coming through the window! I noticed you weren't wearing those dreadful pyjamas though; you were sleeping naked. At least that's some improvement!'

'What? You looked?' Now it was working! Embarrassment and temper were controlling my stutter nicely.

'Why the f…er, why the heck would I want to do that? I saw your pyjamas on the floor, of course!'

'Oh. All right. What are you doing here anyway? Apart from saving me from being beaten up?'

'Can't we get off the street? Don't get me wrong, I'm happy to catch up with you and your thrilling life, and everything, but can't we get comfortable somewhere?'

The pub closed at half past ten; Dokesley was noted for the many cafés and bars it didn't have. Not one. There was only one place to go. Dad was working, on the night shift. Mum would be asleep, and she slept heavily. So, home to twenty-six Whitely Avenue we went. I wanted to do the gentlemanly thing and offer her my arm, but I feared she would make some sarcastic remark. So, I settled for walking along beside her. It was something. It had to be enough.

Elise had fallen quiet and looked pensive. We walked down past the miners' houses, and straight on, on to the council houses of Whitely Avenue. There was a square halfway down the avenue, with a patch of grass, which children played on. It also contained the village's one and only telephone box. She checked her watch.

'One minute,' she considered, 'there's someone I need to try and contact.'

She went into the phone box and dialled a number she had on a piece of paper. She waited for the reply, then pushed four pennies into the slot. They made a satisfying whirr-whirr clang noise as each one went in. I waited outside. She spoke into the mouthpiece, but I couldn't hear what she said. The conversation didn't take long, and she soon rejoined me.

'I thought all you g-guys had radios?'

She shook her head as she emerged from the claustrophobic phone box, 'You watch too many films!'

It was true. *You Only Live Twice* had just come out in our local cinema in Westford. I had been to see it with Tom. It was full of the usual James Bond action, with guns, women and gadgets.

'Anyway. That's done,' she went on, 'can we go?'

We walked on in silence. She was frowning as we walked. There was clearly something on her mind.

I sneaked us into the house, through the back door. I sat her in the living room, then I went into the little kitchen to make coffee. My mother insisted on buying

Co-op's cheap instant coffee. Let's be generous and say it was an acquired taste!

'What the hell is this?' she spluttered after one taste. 'It's bloody awful!'

'Um, we have tea?'

'Any Camomile, Earl Grey, Lapsang Souchong?'

'Erm, what on earth are they? No, Co-op's best only, I'm afraid!'

'Oh, all right. I'm choking for something.'

I went to the 'Caddymatic' tea dispenser. This was a gadget that we had recently bought. It was a cylinder-shaped plastic device, fastened to the wall. It had a tight-fitting lid you could remove, and then you filled it with loose tea leaves. (There were no teabags in those days.) You pushed the button at the bottom, and it dispensed exactly one teaspoon's-worth of tea leaves per push, out of the tapered end. I loved it. I liked gadgets! That was another reason I liked James Bond.

I put three pushes-worth of tealeaves into the teapot and filled it with boiling water from the kettle. I came back to the through lounge, where there was a table at the 'dining' end. We sat at the table and drank tea.

'Well, at least that's a bit better.'

'I'm glad there's something that meets your high standards, milady!'

'I wouldn't go that far!'

Cheeky cat! I thought. I stayed silent and so did she, for quite a while. She seemed to be thinking.

Eventually I was prompted to ask.

'So, what are you doing back here? I know you think it's a dump.'

'So do you!'

'True. But it's *my* dump. I'm entitled! Anyway, I'm stuck here, you're not.'

'My orders were to stay in the area after I'd finished the mission, rather than go back to London. I dropped off the coder at a drop box in Nottingham. I've heard nothing since then. I've been sitting around in my hotel, waiting for further orders. I got bored.' She took a sip of her tea. 'How did you deal with that guy, by the way?'

I told her the story. When I got to the bit about him falling in the river, she laughed. She had a laugh that is best described as unrestrained. She stopped and then she started again. It was infectious. Soon we were both laughing. There was a banging on the ceiling. My mother had woken up and was hitting the floor with her shoe in protest at the noise! She probably thought I was watching a comedy on the telly!

'Shh!' I admonished Elise.

She quietened down to a chuckle. Then she became serious again. She gave me that strange look I had seen twice before. It was hard to describe. It was like she was sizing me up, and actually, to her surprise, finding that I had met some kind of standard. I felt like I had passed a test.

'Weren't you scared? He had a gun,' she

commented.

'I figured it was hard to run and shoot at the same time. So, I ran as fast as I could go.'

'I heard a shot. I was worried about...Well, it was brave. And it meant I could actually search for that bloody thing. It still took me a couple of hours. It was about four o'clock in the morning before I found it. There were no cupboards or anything like that. So, in desperation I went stamping round in all the huts in case there was a hollow floor somewhere. I heard an echoey sound. I hurt my hands trying to get the floorboards up, but I did it in the end. And there it was.'

'What a good idea, to stamp about like that, looking for a hollow spot.'

To my surprise she blushed. So, compliments about her appearance were no good, but compliments about her work, better! I made a mental note.

'My nails were shot to pieces,' she moaned, ruefully, 'I had to chop them afterwards. ' She showed me her hands. Her nails were cut short.

'I think you have nice hands,' I blurted.

'Well, anyway.' She cleared her throat. 'Here I am, stuck here in the flippin' frozen North Midlands, waiting for further instructions.'

'Where are you staying?' I wanted to know.

'There's a hotel not far from here called The Bell, at Bramley. The Service is picking up the bill.'

'OK, but why come back here to Dokesley?' I

persisted.

'Oh, erm, I er, I was bored like I said, and anyway I, er, I wanted to-to have another look at those huts by daylight, in, erm, in case I missed anything...'

Getting information from her was like pulling teeth without any anaesthetic, slow and painful!

I expect they train them not to give anything away, I thought as I sipped my tea in silence.

— CHAPTER SIX —

A Mole in the Hole

'How did you get here?' I asked finally, aware that there were almost no buses.

'Get here? Oh, I came in my car.'

I was jealous. Only seventeen and she had a car? I was very interested in cars; they brought out the nerd in me. 'What is it?' I asked, trying not to sound too eager.

'Oh, it's a Mini.' Minis were the must-have car of 1967. They had been made cool by film stars and pop stars driving them.

'Which model do you drive?'

'Oh, the Cooper S.'

Of course she did! The Mini Cooper S was an iconic car of the age; it had won the Monte Carlo rally earlier that same year. Short of an Aston-Martin DB6, what else would a teenage spy be driving?

'Where is it?'

'It's parked up in the avenue near where I found you. I was driving back from those huts, and I'd just turned off the back lane into Lakefield Avenue when I saw you. Then I saw those two apes, and I thought I'd see how things were.'

'Well, thank you for that... I didn't hear your car.'

'I've had it tuned to be as quiet as possible – and as fast as possible too. It does zero to sixty in ten seconds, and has a top speed of one hundred and forty mph.' She was becoming animated; this was a topic that enthused her. I had met a fellow auto-nerd!

Silence for a while.

'Are you OK?' I asked tentatively, 'Because this is the longest you've gone without a sarcastic comment since I met you!'

She didn't reply for a moment, then she turned to me with a serious face. 'I wasn't going to tell you, but I've just got to tell somebody... but you have to keep it to yourself, OK? It's life and death, do you understand?'

I was taken aback, I nodded solemnly.

'It's like this... You see... I haven't heard from the other trainees,' she blurted out the last phrase, as if glad to get it off her chest, 'We were supposed to meet up after this, our final assignment, for a debrief and a celebration. Our supervisor was going to ring round to say where to meet. I was hoping to be back in London by now, having a great time and a spot of leave. I've heard nothing. I'm worried, if you must know.' She fell silent again.

Wickedly, it crossed my mind, very briefly, that she

might have been deliberately left out of the celebration, because of her sarcastic manner. I knew how that felt; it happened to me a lot when I was growing up. Not invited to birthday parties, or picked for teams, just because I was a bit different. On the other hand, unlike me, she was very attractive, and she was by no means short on personality either. No, this was the sort of girl who would be invited to any parties going. She was right to worry.

'You've not heard from any of them?'

'I wouldn't expect to hear from the other 'babies' – that's what they called us, the babies. There were all sorts of jokes about nappies, and baby bottles…Our only contact is our supervisor. He assigned the tasks, he knew where we all were, no one else did, I wasn't supposed to contact him, none of us were. I was meant to sit in the hotel and wait for the phone call. I sat there for three whole days; just in case he was late for some reason. I've never been so bored in my life! When I didn't hear from him, I was worried. I tried to phone him again just now, as you saw, on the number he gave us for emergencies.' She chewed her bottom lip. 'I wouldn't have expected anyone else to contact me, but I should have been able to get through to him on that emergency number.'

She explained all this, as patiently as she could manage. She didn't have to tell me how worried she was. I could see she was really concerned; it had been half an hour, and counting, since her last sarcastic remark!

'Is there anything I can do?'

She looked at me for a moment. I waited with bated breath for a sarcastic reply, but one never came. 'No, I don't think so, thank you.'

'Is there anything you can do?'

She turned to me and that's when it all burst out of her. She had been storing it up for days.

'I don't know. He was supposed to phone us, to arrange the celebration and meetings, to give us our final assessment grades. I was looking forward to getting my final grade. He's more than three days overdue, so I had to try the emergency number. I called and I asked to speak to him, using his assumed name of Mr Plum.'

I snorted.

'What?'

'Nothing,' I replied, 'go on.'

She gave me a Paddington Bear hard stare before continuing, 'The person at the other end told me she hadn't seen him for a couple of days.' She gave me that look again, the nice one, it made me melt on the spot. 'You know, I actually finished the task early thanks to you! I've been sitting around kicking my heels at the hotel ever since I delivered that damned machine. I decided to come back here. I was, erm, you know, I was retracing my own steps to see if anything, um, occurred to me.' We fell quiet. We drank our tea.

A thought occurred. It was a rare enough

occurrence for me to want to acknowledge it, out loud. I hesitated, then I went for it.

'Erm, Elise?' She looked up in surprise. It was the first time I had used her name. 'Listen, er, you mentioned that there shouldn't have been any foreign agents in the area? You know, when you came here the first time.'

'Yes?'

'Well, why *were* they here? You told me it was, like, a final training exercise. Top secret and all that. No one should have known about it, right?'

'Right. And it's "most secret".'

'Oh, OK. So how *did* they know? Someone must have told them the details of your task.'

She looked at me, thought for a moment and then frowned. Her expression cleared.

'Yes? Yes! Do you know what? I believe you're right!' She slapped me on the back. It was like being hit with a shovel.

'Don't sound so surprised!' I gasped, trying to ease the pain in my back by massaging my shoulder. I was more than a little put out. I had heard that tone of surprise all my life, on the odd occasion I managed to achieve something. Passing the eleven-plus for instance, the only one in my whole primary school class, I might add.

She ignored my remark and continued, speculatively. 'It's true. The chances of that happening on a live operation, especially out here, were minimal. At first,

I sort of assumed they were after the coder, and that the timing was a coincidence... but now I'm beginning to think... I reported their presence to headquarters... I didn't mention you.'

'Why not?'

'To keep you out of it, idiot!' The sarcasm was back, but I could tell her heart wasn't in it.

She fell silent, so did I. We were both thinking hard now. If someone gave the game away, it must have been someone who was close enough to know what her particular mission was, and where it was taking place. She had been betrayed, probably by someone she knew.

'First my mission was compromised, now Sigma One is missing.'

'Ah,' I said, sagely, 'that would be Mr Plum's codename.'

'Give the man a carrot! Actually, it's his rank.'

'What's your rank? Sarky One?' She tried to hide her smile, but I caught it. She recovered her poker face. 'It's Lambda Three, if you must know.'

'Congratulations. If you work hard you might make Lambda Two!'

'Now who's being sarky!'

'You started it!'

'All right, all right. Let's concentrate here. What are we going to do next? That's the question. Stop arguing and start thinking, country boy!'

I took a deep breath. Inside, my heart was just about

ready to burst with happiness. At that moment I didn't care what she called me; she had said 'we', as in 'what are *we* going to do next'. I was over the moon.

'Erm, OK. Could you go back to your, like headquarters, tell them what's happened, and…' I stopped because she was vigorously shaking her head.

'We have to assume I'm blown. That means…'

'I know what it means!' I barked testily.

Again, she ignored me. 'The leak might be at headquarters. It might go all the way to the top. It means that the teen programme is completely compromised, and possibly has been from the very start!' She paused and shook her head. 'I daren't go back until we have more intel. I suppose I don't have to tell you what that means either, film guy!' But this time she smiled. If I'd had a camera, I would have taken a picture, to record that smile! It happened so rarely.

'I can't go back to my hotel tonight; it won't be safe now,' she mused.

'You could stay here,' I suggested, rather too eagerly.

'Don't think for one second I am hiding in your bed again. Once was more than enough!'

'We have a spare bedroom,' I shared as haughtily as I could.

'You'd better lead me to it, then.'

We crept upstairs in silence. I led her to our small spare bedroom on tiptoe, for fear of waking Mum again. She slipped inside, and with a whispered 'Goodnight, country boy!' she closed the door, quietly but firmly. I got ready for bed, then slipped between the sheets. Then I slipped out again, and I took off my pyjamas. I slid back in, wearing nothing but my pants.

I had intended to get up early and cook breakfast for Elise, but when I emerged from my pit, her door was open, and she was gone. The bed was made; it was as if she had never been there, except for a tantalising trace of her scent. I shrugged and went back to bed and instantly fell back to sleep. Mum went out to work without disturbing me, and Dad came in from night shift at the colliery around seven o'clock and went to bed to sleep out the day. I snored on undisturbed.

— CHAPTER SEVEN —
An Agent and One

When I finally awoke, I got dressed, went downstairs and cooked myself some breakfast. I nearly jumped out of my skin when there was a knock on the kitchen window. It was Elise. I let her in the back door.

'I thought I'd better scarper for a bit,' she explained. 'I guessed it would be okay to sneak out at around six o'clock. I thought it would save explanations. I went and sat in my car.'

I looked at her. She'd had about five hours sleep, and looked as fresh as a daisy, whereas I'd had a good eight hours, and I looked like death warmed up!

'I've been thinking…'

'Beginners' luck!' I replied automatically.

'Hey! You're getting better at this sarcasm lark! Good for you, country boy!'

'I do have a name, you know, Lambda Three!'

'No, I don't know. You never told me your name!'

'Oh, oh no, I didn't, did I? Sorry. Well, it's Philip,

Philip Williams.'

She thought about that for a moment, 'Nice to meet you Phil-Will.' I was Phil-Will to her from then on. 'I think we had better begin at Sigma One's base,' she went on, 'If we can find out something about what happened to him, at least it would be a start.'

I got her some breakfast.

'Not bad!' she praised, after she had consumed a huge plateful of bacon, eggs, beans and toast. She looked across at me with one eyebrow raised, impishly. 'So, you can cook, and you can run, is there anything else you can do, Phil-Will?'

'Lots,' I said haughtily, but with those huge green eyes looking at me it was sort of hard to think of anything just then!

She looked amused. 'Can you drive?' she asked.

'A bit.' Dad had been giving me lessons since I turned seventeen, around nine months before. I wasn't bad, on quiet roads.

'OK, you can take turns with me. It's a long drive. When I tried to phone Sigma One, I got the address. It seems it's a boarding house. I was lucky. I got a hotel, of sorts.'

'Wait, I can't just leave! My parents…'

'Leave them a note. I know. Tell them you've been invited away for a few days with a friend. You do have a friend, I suppose?'

'Yes!'

'Well, tell them that. After all it's true enough.'

There was a long pause. I opened and shut my mouth a few times. In the end a kind of madness came over me. At any cost I didn't want to appear a wimp in front of this infuriating, magnificent girl.

'OK, I'll do it. I'll tell them I've gone away with one of my school friends for a bit, camping. I'd better take the camping stuff to make it look realistic.'

'Attaboy! You've got camping stuff?'

I nodded.

'Great. Get it together and bring it, it might come in useful.'

Which is what I did. I tiptoed upstairs, went into the loft and I gathered Dad's old two-man army tent, his ancient sleeping bag, with a spare, and my other camping gear together; as quietly as I could. I didn't want to disturb my father. He was a great Dad, but one thing he couldn't bear was having his sleep disturbed, especially when he had been on night duty. I got some spare clothes, too, and my prehistoric rucksack, inherited from an uncle.

I brought it all downstairs, being careful not to make any more noise than I could help. It took quite a few minutes. When I got back to the living room, I found that Elise had cleaned, washed up and tidied everything in sight. Downstairs, the house looked as neat as a new pin. My parents would be amazed. They would probably attribute it to a guilty conscience – about my sneaking off camping.

Elise inspected the heap of stuff critically. She

looked through the clothes. 'Not exactly at the height of fashion, are we?' she remarked scathingly.

There was no answer to that, except my rather weak reply which was: 'At least mine are clean on today!' It unexpectedly struck a raw spot.

'Ouch, put away your claws, pussycat! I can hardly help that, can I?'

'I will, if you will…you, you tigress!'

Her lips twitched as she suppressed a smile. 'Hmm, not bad! Tigress, eh? I kind of see myself as more of a panther, rawr! But, tigress, OK, I'll take that!' No longer able to suppress the urge, she smiled. 'I'll go and get the car. Can you have everything outside ready?'

'Yeah, I'll just write a note for my parents, like I said.'

She slipped out of the back door and disappeared. I packed all my stuff into my rucksack. Actually, it would be more accurate to say I *stuffed all my pack* into the rucksack. I was trying to be quick.

I composed a brief note to Mum and Dad.

Hi Mum, I got a letter this morning from Mike, at school. He's going camping and wants me to come. I'll be away for a few days. We are going to the peak district. I'll send you a postcard. X

Mike was a good choice. He lived miles away, and, like us, didn't have a phone. It would be next to impossible to check up on me, even if my parents wanted to. I got everything together, including my rucksack and went outside. I waited, and I waited. I looked up the avenue, I looked down the avenue. Nothing. I became concerned. Had she been playing a joke on me all along? Or had something happened? There was nothing to be done, I just had to stand there like a twit and continue hanging on.

In the end Elise made me jump, for the second time that day, as she came up behind me. She must have gone into the fields and back through our garden. At first, I assumed she had crept up on me for a joke, and I was about to say something snide, but the words died on my lips when I saw her expression; she was looking very worried, and she was breathing heavily.

'There are men by my car,' she panted. 'I'm not sure but I think one of them is the man who chased you. They must have been hanging around this area, or they came back for some reason; maybe when they didn't find me at the hotel. They really must have thought you were me! Good job, country boy! They saw my car that night, but only from a distance. I parked it far away. They can't have seen the number. They'll know my face, though. Luckily, they were looking the other way and didn't spot me. If they see me, it's all over. I can't fetch the car while they're there, and they didn't look like moving any time soon.' She bit her lip. She thought. She turned to me. 'Hey, you can drive!' She handed me the car keys. 'Can you get it? Hopefully it might confuse them long enough for you to get back here and pick me up.'

'Hopefully?' I squeaked.

She pursed her lips, as if she was considering the odds for a moment, too long a moment in my opinion! Then she nodded. 'Hopefully,' she repeated, casually.

I hesitated. I had never driven a Mini before, but there were those big, beautiful green eyes, looking up at me.

I swallowed, then squeaked, 'OK.'

'Attaboy!'

Off I went to collect the car. I ran up Whitely Avenue, then slowed to a fast walk. I spotted the Mini at the top of Lakeside. It was white with union flags painted on the roof, bonnet and doors. As I approached, there were indeed three men near the car. One of them came over to me. It was difficult to say, because the last time I saw him it was pitch dark, but I thought I recognised him as the man who chased me that night. I held my breath as he approached.

'Is this your car?' he asked. His English was almost too perfect. He sounded like the Queen.

'Yes, why? Do you like it?'

The man shrugged.

'These cost a lot of money you know,' I boasted proudly, 'zero to sixty in ten seconds, top speed of one hundred and forty. I've had this one tuned up.' I acted as nerdy as I knew how. Behind my back, I crossed my fingers tightly.

To my relief – and my surprise – they stood back while I got in. I had read a phrase somewhere, something like 'a cold sweat bedewed his brow', well it was positively flooding mine and running down my face in icy rivers!

I sat in the driver's seat and tried to look as though I knew what I was doing. By some miracle the car started first time. Luckily the gears were not so different from the Hillman Minx, which was my dad's car. In those days Hillman, Morris, and Austin – who made the Mini Cooper – were all under the same umbrella: the British Motor Corporation.

I managed to drive away smoothly enough. She was right. They were sufficiently confused to let me get away; they must have been persuaded that this wasn't the Mini they were looking for. They stood on the pavement talking, not even looking at me as I drove off.

I drew up at our house feeling rather triumphant. I rolled down the window, 'Your carriage awaits, milady.'

She joined in the by-play. She pretended to stick her nose in the air, 'Carry on, Williams!'

'Erm, I think it's best if you drive,' I hesitated, 'Um, you know, to start with.'

She looked at me for a moment. 'OK, you can take your turn later.'

'Where are we going?'

'Cornwall.'

'Cornwall?' I gasped. We'd had a holiday in Falmouth when I was eleven. The journey was engraved on my memory – it had taken forever to get there. This was not the age of motorways. There was the M1 and that was pretty much it! Apart from bits and pieces that were largely called 'by-passes' for this or that town. There was no M5, for example, no M3, and no M6.

'Don't worry. This thing can move.'

'It's not the moving that worries me, it's the stopping suddenly!'

'Stow your gear and get in. Which way do we go? Is there another way out of this wretched village? They might be watching the main road.'

I had hardly closed the door when she shot off down the road. I was jolted down into my seat and had to fight my way upright.

'T-turn left!' I gasped as we reached the end of the avenue. She performed a racing turn, and the nimble little car roared down the road towards the Nissen huts and the air raid shelters. The route to the right was the obvious route to the main road. Going left would evade any prying eyes, and it should give us a good head start, supposing we survived her driving!

It was a one-track country road with overtaking places. Down the road a way, I got her to turn into a lane on the right, the entrance almost hidden if you didn't know where it was.

'Are you sure about this?' She asked, her voice

quavering in time with the bouncing of the Mini, as we clattered down what was little more than a bridle path.

'Keep going. Aargh!' The Mini took off over a bump. 'But maybe slow down a bit,' I cried in alarm.

She shrugged, but she did slow down – a little. Sure enough, the lane came out into a lay-by, by the side of the main road. She stopped the car for a moment, but kept the engine revving.

'Score one for Phil-Will!' she said with a smile. 'So where to now?'

'Erm, have you got a map?'

'I thought you said you'd been to Cornwall?'

'Once. When I was eleven. I wasn't paying much attention to the road. I know there was this enormously steep hill, and we had to get out and walk, because the car was overloaded.'

She sighed. I felt terrible. Then she smiled. I felt wonderful.

'If *I* don't know the way, I can't blame you, can I? All right, the map's in the door pocket.'

I got it out. It was one of those maps you always see in comedies. It unfolded like a six-dimensional concertina.

'Well, er, this is the A1, and we need to go south. We need the A5, I think.'

'See what you can do when you try!'

— CHAPTER EIGHT —
Agent on the Trail

She pulled out of the lay-by, and off we went. A few short days ago I had lain in bed and wished I could spend more time with Elise. Now I was going to have my wish, 'in spades,' as they used to say in the American gangster films. I was in a dream, and it was a good one. I sneaked a look at her as she focused on driving. She frowned slightly when she was concentrating, and she made this adorable little pout. My heart was singing.

We had to head north to start with; the dual carriageway at this point meant we could only turn left. We headed for the roundabout where five roads met, so as to turn around. I looked at the map again, and I realised I had chosen the wrong route! We were approaching the roundabout at high speed. This girl drove like a rally driver!

'Where now?'

'Erm, change of plan we need to head for Mansfield then it's the A38 all the way to Bodmin.'

'Are you *sure* this time?' Sarky One had returned!

'Yes. Look… NO, DON'T LOOK! It's on the map. Mansfield. Take the first…too late! OK, go round the roundabout again, then take that road there, there, to Mansfield!'

We were on our way. It was a long drive. The Mini's seats were relatively comfortable, but I was nonetheless stiff and sore after a while. From time to time Elise let me drive just to give her a rest, but she could see I wasn't confident. Especially when I took out my glasses and put them on. I needed them for driving. To her eternal credit she never said a word about my driving. She even closed her eyes, when it was my turn to drive; although between me and you, I couldn't work out if this showed confidence in me or whether it was sheer terror!

When three hours had gone by, we paused for a rest and something to eat. We stopped at a roadside café, the type of place we used to call a 'greasy spoon'. These were fairly basic establishments, meant as truck stops. The food was plain, but plentiful. She treated me to a pork chop with chips. She had something similar.

Soon she was anxious to be off. She grabbed my arm and dragged me out to the car. I was still finishing my cup of tea, but I didn't care. It was the first physical contact of any kind since that light kiss on the cheek in the rain on the night we met. Progress, hooray! I wiped the spilled tea from my jumper, and on we went.

It was my turn to drive for a bit. I was getting more and more confident as time went by. This was turning out to be the longest driving lesson I had ever had. And the best bit was that no one was shouting at me!

'You know I've only got my provisional licence, don't you? If the police stop us...'

'Don't speed, we'll be fine. Besides, I've got my full licence, we'll just tell them the L plates must have fallen off. Tell you what, if you're worried, we'll stop in the next town and get some.' So, we did. The next town was Alveston, and there was a garage where we could get the magnetic L plates for the front and back of the car. We got a cup of coffee in a local café, and I used the loo. Once again, she paid for everything.

L-plates in place, we set off once more for all points south-west. Finally, at around six o'clock on a warm evening, we arrived in Bodmin. Bodmin was once the county town of Cornwall. Despite its important history, it was no bigger than Westford. This was our destination. Sigma One's last known address was here. We parked in the main street and bought an *A to Z* map book of the local area from a newsagent's shop.

'Not bad, Phil-Will,' Elise gushed. 'Your navigation was spot on, just like that night in the fields. So, runner, cook and navigator. I'm wondering what other talents we might find!' To be honest, so was I! I'd never seen myself as having any talents before. I said nothing. I just smiled, in what I thought was a nonchalant manner.

'Are you all right? You were pulling a funny face!'

'I'm fine!' I replied, a bit testily.

She looked up the address of Mr Plum's lodgings in the *A to Z*. It was in one of the little streets nearby. We walked there, leaving the car parked in the high street. As she had said, it was a boarding house. She hesitated, and we stood outside, just looking at the place. It was a big Victorian house, with about four floors. There was a sign in the window: 'Vacancies'.

Elise took a deep breath. 'OK, here we go.'

The door was open. We went in. It looked just like any typical big house of that time. There was a hallway with doors off both sides, and a staircase going up to the upper floors. The floor was covered with lino, a shiny plastic floor covering, but the staircase was covered with a 'runner' a stair carpet that ran up the middle of the steps, with painted wood visible either side. It was rather threadbare. The place was in need of decoration, and it smelled of cabbage. Why did boarding houses always smell of boiled cabbage? The whole effect was rather depressing. There was a tiny counter in one corner of the hallway. A faded notice read 'reception'. There was a bell. She rang it.

A woman emerged from a back room somewhere and came over to us, wiping her wet hands on a tea towel. Running a boarding house was hard work, and it showed in her face and body. She was a remarkably tall woman, thin, and with her hair drawn back into a tight bun. Her face looked severe, but she had a sweet smile. She looked at the two of us. When neither of us spoke, she did, in a strong Cornish accent:

'I've a double room on the third floor,' she drawled. 'Hot water is between seven and ten in the morning only. The bathroom is at the end of the corridor. There's a W.C next to it. It's fifteen shillings a night…' She looked at the two of us again, 'Each! And no questions asked.'

Elise and I looked at one another, and I blushed. Elise gave a twisted smile.

'Erm, no. Er, hello,' Elise began. 'Mrs Trevannion? I called earlier to enquire about my, my friend. You said you hadn't seen him for a while.'

'Oh, yes. I remember. You called from a phone box? Mr Plum. I remembered, because of the funny name, like that game, you know, *Cluedo*.' Elise smiled, thinly. 'Yes,' the lady went on, 'well, he was away for a day or two, like I told you on the phone, but he's come back, my love. This morning. Came back all muffled up, poor dear. Toothache, apparently.'

Elise's face relaxed for the first time since we'd arrived in Cornwall. She positively beamed. 'Oh good!' she exclaimed. 'I'm so relieved. I suppose that's why he hasn't been in touch. Can I see him?'

Jealous thoughts filled my mind.

'Room six, my dear, on the second floor,' Mrs Trevannion said, before disappearing back into the beyond.

Elise was about to run off up the stairs when I grabbed her arm.

'Elise,' I hissed. 'Haven't you ever seen any spy films? Don't they show you *James Bond* as part of your training?'

'No, they don't, and no I haven't!' she hissed back. 'What do you mean?'

This was turning into another hissing match. I pulled her to one side away from the bottom of the stairs.

'Think! He came back all muffled up? He couldn't speak properly "because of his tooth"?' She looked blankly at me. 'It's not him! It's someone pretending to be him!'

'You don't know that!' she scoffed.

'I think it's worth considering, don't you?'

She thought. Her face clouded over. There was that lovely pout again. 'I do see what you mean. I suppose I was so eager to see him; I didn't think…'

'Of course, and they are probably counting on that. I bet you are not the first member of the team to come here looking for him. Where are *they* now?'

Now she got it. I must say, when she realised the truth she reacted with remarkable speed and resolution. 'We need to get into that room. If he's hurt Sigma One…'

A spike of jealousy reared up and struck me in the chest. 'You *like* him, don't you?'

'I admire him,' she claimed, then bit her lip as I gazed at her. Blushing, she looked down, then back up at me. She sighed. 'All right, I had a crush on him. I really liked him, and I thought he liked me.' Her face briefly crumpled, and I saw pain pass across her expression. Her eyes began to glisten as she sighed and took a deep breath. 'Don't worry, it was just a stupid teenage crush.' She bit her lip. 'Anyway, he's a lot older than me, if you know what I mean. I'm, I'm over it.' A fugitive tear gave away the lie in that remark; she brushed it away angrily.

I said nothing, but I could feel my heart sinking southward towards my shoes, and the painful ache of jealousy. I knew I was being unfair and irrational, but I didn't care, I really liked this girl.

She turned to the stairs again, and for the second time I had to restrain her. 'Wait! You can't just go charging in, we need a plan!'

She thought about the situation. I watched her face change.

'All right. So, what do you suggest, *plan boy*?'

I was flattered. She was asking *me*! A little sarcastically perhaps, but nonetheless. My heart, back in my chest again, swelled in response. I deliberated.

'We need a way to get into the room, or to get him out of it,' I answered thoughtfully.

'We could ring the fire alarm!' she exclaimed, she was just itching to do it, too.

'That's a bit messy, isn't it?' I queried.

'Well, what do you suggest? Do you have a better idea?'

'How about something really simple?'

'Coming from you, that seems appropriate!' she quipped. 'OK, like what?'

'Like, we go up to his door and…Yes, that's it. We ask if he needs any more pillows or something. Then when he opens the door you grab him and do your judo thing.'

She considered. 'You know, that might work. I like simple. Come on then, simple Simon.'

I followed her up to the second floor.

CHAPTER NINE

An Agent Found

Iwas about to watch a little masterpiece of acting. Elise rapped on the door of room number six peremptorily, as if she had every right to be there.

'Sir, sir,' she cried out, in a remarkably good imitation of the landlady's Cornish accent. 'Sir is there anything you need? I have some brandy for your tooth...'

The brandy was a neat touch. Who would refuse free booze?

There was the sound of someone approaching the door. She winked at me and indicated I should get out of sight. I nipped around the corner, but I couldn't resist peeping.

The man opened the door. He was caught completely off guard. He was surprised to be met, not by the landlady, but a teenage girl with a big smile. She was ready with her hands linked in a double fist, and off to one side. The fists came round at speed and got him with pinpoint accuracy right in the solar plexus. His breath escaped from him with a sort of whooshing noise, and he folded over. He was completely winded and temporarily helpless. I winced as Elise brought up her knee and gave him a real wallop on the chin. His head went back, and he went down like a sack of potatoes.

'Ow!' Elise cried, hobbling around for a moment or two. 'Ow, ow, OW! That hurt. They didn't tell us about that bit.' She rubbed her sore leg for a minute. Then it was back to business. 'Help me,' she hissed.

I ran to her and helped her drag the man inside the room. It was a standard, common or garden boarding house bedroom, with a narrow bed, an easy chair and a small table with two dining chairs.

'You know,' I decided. 'I really, really wouldn't want to have you mad at me!'

'I came second in the class at unarmed combat.'

'Only second? I really wouldn't want to meet the guy who came first!'

'He used to cheat.'

She went to the wardrobe and found some neckties, probably belonging to the room's official occupant, Sigma One himself. I peeked over her shoulder at the clothes in the wardrobe.

'I suppose you like *his* clothes sense.' The little green monster inside me would not be quiet.

'As a matter of fact, I do. He always dresses beautifully.'

There were no casual clothes in those days, things

were gradually changing, but jackets and ties were still worn even in casual situations. She was very business-like as she trussed up the poor unconscious man with the ties, then fastened one tightly round his mouth.

'I suppose they teach you knots at spy school.'

'No, I learned that in the girl guides.'

She left him there, very effectively bound and gagged, while she searched the room for clues.

'I, er, I take it that this isn't—'

'No, it isn't,' she snapped. 'You were right, OK? Well done you.' She stopped, hung her head and sighed. 'I'm sorry, Phil. I'm sorry. You were right, and you probably saved my life. I was just going to barge in. God knows what would have happened if you hadn't been here to pull me back. Look. I'm worried, scared and confused. I apologise, OK? Come here.' And she actually came over and gave me a hug.

I hugged her back enthusiastically. 'It's OK,' I said, breathing in her scent and enjoying the feel of her hair against my face.

She pulled away and was suddenly all business-like. 'Right. Ahem. Let's see if there is anything to help us before we start to interrogate this one.'

We began to search the room. I couldn't believe this. This was real James Bond stuff. All my fantasies were coming true.

'What's that next to the phone?' I asked, as we worked.

'Can't you guess, film-boy?' she replied with a little

smile. I shook my head.

'It's a scrambler, to make sure phone conversations are secure.'

'Oh, OK.'

I looked around the room. What should I do? What would 007 do? He would frisk the unconscious man, that's what. I searched the man's clothing. I stopped and gaped at what I found in one of his trouser pockets. A pistol of some kind, I had never handled, never even seen, a real gun in my whole life. I stared at it for a moment, then, to free up my hands for further searching, I put it in my own pocket. His jacket was hanging on a chair, and I went through that next. There were various papers, a French passport and a wallet. The wallet had both English and foreign money. I waved one of the foreign notes under Elise's nose. She turned from a drawer she was rootling in. She took the money and looked at it. I couldn't read the writing at all, but it was no problem for her:

She read it out loud. 'Sovietska roobless' was what it sounded like to me. 'Roubles,' she said,' Russian money. So now at least we're sure who we're dealing with.' She swallowed hard. She took a deep breath and paused for a moment. Then she stuck out her chin determinedly. It was the second time I had seen it. I loved it when she did that.

Elise had shown a moment of temporary weakness, as she realised what we were up against – the full might and cunning of the USSR, the Soviet Union.

Their reputation for ruthlessness was well known. Her weakness soon passed, and she was all business-like again. *My* weakness, on the other hand, was just kicking off its shoes and settling in for a while – it had come for a long stay! The reality of it had not struck me until now. We were really going up against armed Russians! My legs had turned to rubber. I had to sit down for a moment. I took a chair at the table and put my head between my legs; very un-Bond-like.

Elise either didn't notice, or she pretended not to. 'Right, come on. Let's see what we've got.' She sat next to me. I sat up, took some deep breaths, and we pooled our findings. There was very little from her search.

'If he had time, Sigma One would have hidden any papers or destroyed them.'

'And if he didn't have time?'

'Then, they've got all the mission information and contact details for our whole team… Wait… That must be how they found me in the first place. My mission was compromised from the beginning…' She stood, frozen, with a horrified look on her face. She had come to a startling conclusion. 'They never wanted the coder, they just wanted to catch me! That means, that means, this was all about… Oh God, the others…' Her face paled, and she put her hand up to her mouth.

'Elise, we don't know what happened to the others,' I tried to reassure her. I hated seeing her upset like this. I attempted to distract her. 'But how did they find your car? Why were they even in Dokesley today?'

'I think they went to my hotel, and when I wasn't there, they lost track of me. They were on a fishing expedition. If I hadn't come to see...ahem...' She paused, cleared her throat and started again. 'That is if I hadn't come to your village, I might have been captured or even killed at the hotel.'

I had been listening hard, mainly because I loved the sound of her voice when she spoke. It was unusual for me to pay so much attention to someone. I had noticed something as a result.

'Whoa, whoa, back it up, sister!' I exclaimed. 'What did you "come to see"?' She looked quizzically at me. I ploughed on growing less and less confident in the spotlight glare of her poker-faced stare. 'You said you "came to see" and then you sort of stopped,' I finished, lamely.

'You don't miss much do you? Except maybe the big picture.' There was that look of pleased surprise again. I was emboldened to try again.

'We-ell, you already got the coder thing, you didn't come to see the huts again, you didn't come to look at the kale field, I'm pretty sure. In fact, if I didn't know better, I might have thought you were going to say... you came back to see *me*,' I said, getting a piece of the big picture. Finally.

'You know, you're slow, but you get there in the end, don't you!' And she gave me that look again. I melted inside. If I had been a dog, I would have been wagging my tail.

'You came back to see *me*?'

'Is this the time?' she said. She was blushing like a red traffic light. I knew a stop sign when I saw one. I shut up. But my heart was soaring. She really had come back to see me! Wow. Me. Lonely, friendless, nerdy, me.

I remembered the gun. I cleared my throat. 'Oh, I found this, in his pocket.' I offered it to her. She lit up like a Christmas tree.

'Golly,' she said in her posh accent, an accent which I couldn't stand before, but which – for some reason – I now adored.

'It's a Makarov pistol, a real one. I've only ever seen replicas,' she said with the same reverence that other women might say 'it's a diamond bracelet' or 'it's a Cartier watch'.

'I know what to get you for your birthday then,' I joked.

'Yes, please.' She examined the gun as a jeweller would examine a priceless ruby. It might have been my imagination, but it seemed to me that even her voice mellowed, as she caressed the lethal hardware.

She took it to pieces right then and there and reassembled it. I watched open-mouthed. I'd not seen anyone's hands move as cleverly, since seeing the magician David Nixon doing one of his tricks on the telly.

She saw me gaping and shrugged. 'Oh, I came top of the class in sidearms.'

'I can see why.'

'This is an amazing gun. Nine-millimetre blowback design. Based on the Walter PP.'

'Walter PP? That's James Bond's gun! Wow.'

She gave me a look, but ignored me and carried on. 'It is light enough for pretty much anyone to use, it packs a real punch, and it's small enough to go in a handbag.'

'Somehow I can't see you with a handbag!'

She went on as if she hadn't heard me. 'The only problem is the first shot. It takes a real squeeze of the trigger to fire the first one. After that, you can fire as quick as you like.' She looked at the gun reverently again, then pointed it at the wall and pretended to shoot. She made 'kapow' noises, pretending to shoot the lamp, the pillows and her reflection in the mirror. 'He must be military, it's a military issue weapon. This is a great find; it tells us a lot. Good job, Phil-Will.'

'Please be careful, Elise,' I begged, ducking as she waved the gun around.

'I know what I'm doing! It's perfectly safe to carry with the safety engaged…' She examined it again. 'Oh. Well, it's safe with the hammer at rest, as well.' She put the safety catch on.

'Should I leave you two alone?' I quipped.

— CHAPTER TEN —
An Agent Dies

She slipped the pistol into her pocket and cleared her throat, 'Right; what now, Phil-Will?'

That was a good question. I had no idea what to do next.

I stalled for time. 'What do *you* think?'

'Wait a minute, I've just thought of something.' She went to the drawer she had been looking in when I interrupted her. She pulled it right out and turned it over. There was an envelope sellotaped to the underside of the drawer. Excitedly she ripped it off and felt inside. Her face fell when she found it empty. Or almost empty. At the bottom she found a small, folded piece of paper. It looked blank.

'There's nothing there,' I groaned, peering into the envelope.

'I'm not sure,' she mused. 'Let's see.' She went across to the lamp, turned it on and held the piece of paper over the bulb. It must have burned her hands, but she held it there long enough for blurred letters and numbers to form, revealed by the heat.

It was a telephone number and a single word. 'Whirlwind.'

'Don't tell me,' I remarked, 'you were top of the class in codes and secret writing.'

She smirked. 'Something like that.' She then sucked her poor, burned fingers.

'But where does it get us?' I asked.

'It's a London dialling code,' she said indistinctly, through a mouthful of fingers. 'That word is obviously a password of some kind. The opposition ignored it because they thought it was just a scrap of paper.'

'But you knew better! Good job, Lambda Three.'

She looked at me. 'You know, we make a good team.'

Something seemed to be affecting my throat. 'Yes, ahem, yes! Thank you! I think we do.' I gulped, taken aback by a genuine compliment from top-of-the-class, sarcastic, spy-girl.

'Don't go all gooey on me, Phil-Will. We have work to do.'

'Gooey? I, er, I don't know what you mean. Ahem. What are you going to do?'

'I think we should find a telephone box and ring this number, don't you? And you can say the password. Have you got any pennies?'

'It's going to take more than pennies to ring London from here.'

'Well, sixpences then, half crowns, anything?'

We pooled our monetary resources. While we were doing this there was a sound from the corner of the room. It was the man she had tied up. He groaned and then collapsed. The blood drained from Elise's face; she went as white as a sheet. She hurried over to him.

'Bloody hell, he's taken poison! It must have been hidden in a tooth. I should have thought of that.'

'He's dead?' I squeaked. 'A-Are you sure?'

I was shocked out of my wits. So far, I had been concentrating on trying to please this amazing girl, the girl who had stolen my heart so completely. That was the real reason I had gone with her. Up to this point, it had been like a game, like one of my James Bond fantasies; it had been fun. Now here was this man, who had killed himself. Had decided to actually commit suicide, rather than be taken prisoner. It wasn't a game anymore. It was no longer fun. I stared at her, horrified.

'B-Bloody hell!' I thought the occasion merited a swear word.

'Isn't this exciting?' she jabbered. 'You're even learning how to swear!' She peered over the dead man's body. 'Oh, why did he do that? We haven't even covered physical interrogation techniques yet, so I wouldn't have hurt him.'

'But you might have called someone who would.'

'Do you realise what this means? The stakes must be…'

'Really high.' I finished her sentence for her.

'C'mon, give me a hand.' She started to undo the

neckties around his wrists. Following her example, I did his ankles. We removed his gag, and then put him on the bed. I had never seen a dead person before, let alone helped carry one. As we dropped him down, he made a noise. I almost leapt right out of my skin. It sounded like an old teddy bear's growl. The last bit of air had been forced out of his dead lungs as we moved him, causing his vocal chords to vibrate.

I wasn't enjoying this one bit. I dropped his legs just as they were, wrenched the bedroom door open and ran off to the bathroom down the hall. I only just managed to hold on to the contents of my stomach before I reached the toilet. A few minutes later, having cleaned up after myself, I came back, green about the gills and feeling rotten.

'It's my first ever dead person,' I groaned, as we person-handled him straighter on the bed. To my relief he made no more noises.

'How many corpses do you think *I've* seen?'

I looked at her white face. 'Exactly one?'

'Correct! We need to get out of here, *pronto*,' she said. 'His friends might call at any moment.'

We left him there on the bed, looking for all the world as though he were asleep. We then left the room and closed and re-locked the door; Elise pushed the key under it. The whole episode had taken less than ten minutes.

Elise thanked Mrs Trevannion nicely.

'I tried his room, but I couldn't get an answer. He's

probably sleeping off his toothache,' said Elise.

'What were you doing up there then?'

'Oh, we both had to use the bathroom,' I extemporised.

'I hope you left it as you found it!'

'Of course,' I said, forestalling the possibility of sarcastic remarks from my companion. I was used to going to boarding houses on holiday with Mum and Dad. I'd met any number of hardworking house-proud landladies like this, scraping a living for themselves when their husbands didn't come back from the Second World War.

I wasn't sure she was convinced; goodness knows what she suspected we had been doing for that time. Whatever her guesses might have been, they would certainly have been wide of the mark! Anyway, she was pleasant enough when we said goodbye.

We got outside onto the pavement. I leaned against the wall for a moment. Then I said, somewhat desperately, 'Speaking of using the bathroom...'

'You're not going to be sick again, are you?'

'No! I need to, you know, *use the bathroom.*'

'Oh, oh I see. You need to pee. Actually, so do I.'

I'd never met a girl so forthright. Actually, I'd never really been alone with a girl for this long, ever. When it came to girls I had been relying on pre-conceived ideas culled from books. I had this crazy notion they were soft and gentle creatures who needed to be looked after by manly men – which was a problem for me – I had always felt somewhat inadequate manliness-wise.

Well, so much for that idea! My pre-conceived notions were being turned upside down. Here was a woman who didn't need looking after. If anything, I was beginning to see that my role would be holding her back from doing ever more dangerous and impetuous things.

This forthrightness of hers made life a lot easier. I felt I could talk to her about just about anything, and she wouldn't be upset or offended. Anyway, when you've dealt with a dead body together, anything afterwards should be a piece of cake.

— CHAPTER ELEVEN —
Whirlwind

We went back towards the car and spotted a café on the way. I quickly got over my nausea, and I was now hungry. We headed for the café like twin food-seeking missiles. The café was not a luxurious place. We had dinner there and used the bathrooms. The food was OK. I had steak and kidney pie with chips, and a cup of tea. Elise had steak and chips and coffee. She pulled a face at the coffee. 'I should have had tea,' she remarked. After the meal, it was time to make the phone call.

There was a telephone in the café. It was in the gloomy, ill-lit corridor that led to the toilets. The wall all around the phone was covered in scrawled phone numbers and other graffiti. Stale cooking smells lingered in the passageway, not to mention toilet smells. The ubiquitous lino was on the floor, broken and worn in places. It was not nice. Elise didn't turn a hair.

She stood her stack of coins by the phone and rang

the number on the slip of paper we found.

'It stinks in here,' I said, conversationally.

'Oh, this is nothing. I once had to hide in a sewer pipe on an exercise.' She gave me a sideways look. 'And once in someone's bed, while they were in it! Ah. They're answering...' She put some money in the slot and pressed button A. The coins disappeared with a clunking sound.

She held the phone so that we could both hear it. A woman's voice answered. 'Do you have a weather report for me?' Elise dug me in the ribs.

Taken by surprise, I stammered: 'W-Whirlwind!'

'Putting you through.'

Elise covered the mouthpiece with her hand. 'It worked,' she whispered delightedly.

Another woman came on the phone:

'Sigma One? You're late reporting back. I was getting worried. Go to scrambler.'

Elise took over, 'Hello, this is Lambda Three, reporting.'

'Lambda Three? What are you doing there? This is not a secure line. Do you not have a scrambler?'

'Negative.' She looked at me and shrugged. I shrugged back. 'OK, I'll just have to be as discreet as I can.' She thought for a moment and then continued. 'I pulled off the final, er business deal for my branch of the firm, but it was against a surprising amount of opposition, I repeat much opposition. I waited some time but when I hadn't heard anything, and messages were overdue, I came to er, to branch headquarters looking for the manager; only to find that he had er, gone away and a takeover had occurred. There was, there was a caretaker manager there from the opposing firm. He, er, he was so surprised to see me that he fainted clean away, repeat clean away.'

'Understood. Is he still there?'

'Yes.'

I listened to this with admiration and confusion in equal amounts. I understood some of it, missed some of it, but I admired all of it. It was as if Elise was improvising a play, on the spot!

'I need you to leave that location immediately. I will see to a cleaning firm for the branch headquarters. Can you take a holiday for a while? I can't help you, as I need to er, to get my head down.'

'All right, but is there nothing I can do?'

'Nothing safe.'

'That wasn't what I asked.'

There was a pause at the other end of the phone.

'Are you alone?'

'No.'

'Thought so, I can hear breathing.' I put my hand over my mouth. The voice went on, 'Member of the firm?'

'No.'

'A civilian? That's not good, Lambda Three.'

'He saved my life, twice.'

'Very well. Your other branch members?'

'Unknown.'

'Did they complete their, their work projects?'

'Unknown.'

'I have no information that they did.' A pause, then the voice went on, 'Very well. We have to assume for now that you are the only branch member still working. Make your way to the Snake Inn Hotel, Derbyshire. Information will be waiting for you. And for heavens' sake take care. Trust no one. Repeat, no one. From now on your call sign will no longer be Lambda Three; it will be Sigma One until further notice. I'll send you a list of safe houses. I will phone each of them in turn, regularly until I reach you, or until I receive... other news.' The phone went dead.

Elise gave a happy sigh at her promotion, as she put the phone down. 'Sigma One!' she exclaimed. 'I've been made Sigma One.' Her face changed. She frowned and then she turned to me. 'Look, Phil. Erm, what do you think?' she asked, as she led the way back to our seats.

I was still thinking about that 'other news', but I came out of my reverie. 'Oh. I think you were incredible!' I gushed. 'All that stuff about the branch and the branch manager and... Amazing! But what's "fainted clean away"?'

'Oh, that's service-speak for brown bread, you know, dead,' she explained as we took our seats.

'OK. Well, you were just fantastic.'

She blushed. 'Oh, erm thank you.' She tucked away

96

a loose strand of hair. 'But that wasn't what I meant. Do you think we should do what she said? Do you think it's safe to go on with this?'

'Do you care if it's safe? '

'I... I care about you. You're not trained for this.'

'I'm learning fast. Besides, I'm with *you*, aren't I? What could go wr... Wait... you *care* about me?'

'Well, I, I just wouldn't want to see you hurt. Obviously.' She fiddled with her hair again, and she buried her face in her coffee cup.

'You care about *me*!'

'All right, I care about you, OK? There! You forced me to say it.'

I didn't have to force very hard, was my unspoken thought. I quashed it. I felt wonderful.

She paused, for quite a while, before she continued in a confidential manner. 'Look. Every boy I've ever met has been put off by me and my me-ness! You were the first one who answered me back. You didn't care how much I insulted you, and you stuck with me even when it was dangerous. God knows I didn't want this to happen. I didn't want to have feelings for you, I fought it. But it was no good. And now I feel responsible for you.' She was breathing heavily after this little speech.

'I hope you don't still see me as a millstone.' I was getting hot under the collar for more than one reason. My emotions were thoroughly confused, but the overwhelming feeling was one of soaring, sparkling joy. She cared for me. *She cared for me!*

'Of course not, oh, Phil, you've been a brick. I might have been captured, or even dead right now if not for you; and I couldn't have completed my assignment.' She grabbed my hand across the table tightly and looked into my eyes. I considered whether a brick was better than a millstone, but as she held my hand, I supposed it was! She looked away and gave my hand one last squeeze before letting go. I could see there were tears in her eyes.

'Look what you've done to me.' She sniffed, blew her nose on a handkerchief, wiped away her tears and laughed. She looked at me and smiled. 'Well, what are you waiting for, let's go!'

'We need to find somewhere to sleep,' I said, 'it's getting late.' It was nine o'clock by now, and the sun was setting. The last vestiges of light were leaving the sky over Bodmin.

'I think we should avoid hotels and things.'

'We have the camping gear,' I suggested. 'There's a phone box over there, we could look up a campsite in the yellow pages.'

'If it's still there,' she said cynically. 'People steal the phone books from the phone boxes.'

Luckily, the yellow pages book was still there. I found a campsite on Bodmin Moor. I showed her.

'OK. You're the navigator. So, navigate!'

She jumped into the car, and I had barely time to get in before she was off. I had to pull the door shut at around thirty miles an hour. There were, of course, no seatbelts at this time, not in this car anyway. And, before you ask, definitely no airbags. It was a different time. After a struggle I righted myself, and we were off again.

— CHAPTER TWELVE —
An Agent and One in a Tent

Elise was in the mood to share as she drove, looking steadfastly ahead out of the car windscreen, 'I was one of only two girls in the teenage-trainee programme. The other one dropped out pretty quickly. That left me on my own with a load of male chauvinist teen boys, and all their male hormones. The only way I could manage the situation was by being "one of the boys". I had to swear more, run faster, shoot better, and do all the assignments better than them, just to keep my place. It wasn't fair, but I did it anyway.' There was pride in her voice, and I couldn't blame her.

She continued, briskly. 'One or two of them tried it on, but I was concentrating on doing well on the course. There was the odd one I might have liked, but I put people off with my manner. I don't know how to speak to boys! In the end I didn't date any of them.'

I thought hard for a few moments. 'Turn left at the next junction, then it's a straight road for six miles... are you sure that was the reason why you didn't, you know, get dates?'

'What do you mean?'

'Don't get me wrong, you are *not* what I expect a girl to be, and I do see what you are saying, about your "me-ness", your Elise-ness. But maybe there is something else.'

'Mmm?' she encouraged as she peered into the dusk, watching the road. We were going through the countryside now, and she had the headlights on full beam. They lit up the road ahead, and the rather bleak, but beautiful moorland on either side.

'I mean,' I went on. 'Look, don't get mad, but I think it might be like this. Say I saw you, like in a pub or something, I wouldn't even try to ask for a date. You're, well... you're just so... so...'

'So? "So" what? Unapproachable, aloof, what?'

'Well...' I blushed. 'So lovely to look at,' I mumbled.

'Eh? OK, but why would that stop you? Surely you should be all the more eager? Come on, I really want to know!'

'Well, look at you, then look at me. You're really pretty, you're confident... Then look at me, I've got spots, specs and I'm skinny... and I stammer. I would never try to date a girl like you. I wouldn't stand a chance! She would laugh in my face.'

'Maybe not.'

'Ha!'

She drove quietly for a while, that delightful thinking pout of hers appeared.

'All right. What's my most attractive feature would you say?'

Oh God. Now I was completely out of my depth. I thought about it. I'd complimented her on her looks once before; I experienced her razor-sharp sarcasm as a result! I was determined not to fall into that trap again.

'Um, erm…' I stammered.

'Come on, you said I'm attractive, I don't see it. What's my most attractive part?'

After a long silence I plucked up the courage to answer, 'Erm. Your bravery, your amazing, like can-do-ness. Your physical skills.'

'Yeah, yeah, but you didn't know any of that at first. What's the first attractive thing you noticed about me; I mean about the way I look?'

I was flustered, she had backed me into a corner. I thought. I sweated. Then I remembered that night in my bedroom all those days ago. I had it!

'You really want to know?' I ventured. She nodded.

'Actually…'

'Yes, yes?'

'The first thing I noticed was your figure, silhouetted against the window. You, you have a lovely figure.'

'Oh! OK. OK, I'll take that. I'll take that; because I've worked hard on my figure.'

Phew, I felt I'd dodged a bullet there!

'That's really why I didn't shout for help. I could see at once you were a girl.'

'Give the boy a carrot!'

'Hey, welcome back, Sarky One! So, what was it about me? Was it my spots, my specs, or perhaps my stammer?'

'Do you really want to know?' She smiled broadly, as she stared ahead, then she began to giggle.

'Go on.' I sighed.

'It was those ridiculous pyjamas.'

'My pyjamas?'

'Yes. I thought that was really endearing. Then afterwards, of course, I found out about the other stuff. About how brave *you* are, and your running, and your cooking of course!'

'Look out, it's just coming up, ahead.'

'And your navigation skills!' she added, as she turned the wheel; we screeched around the corner and headed up the drive in the fading twilight.

We pulled up at the campsite office, just as the last faint glow of daylight disappeared from the horizon. That ended the conversation. Elise negotiated the fiscal formalities in the site office.

She came back to the car shaking her head. 'Ten shillings a night for us and the car! It's daylight robbery!' (Ten shillings is fifty pence in modern money.)

'Can't be daylight robbery, it's night-time.'

'Don't be pedantic! He said we park the car in the car park here, then we can put the tent up anywhere over there'. She waved in the general direction of a group of tents near a hedge. 'The showers-and-toilets block is just there.' She indicated a bleak-looking concrete building behind the campsite offices.

Between us we managed to erect the two-person tent. Elise had a toolbox in the car, which contained, amongst other things, a hammer. The ground had not been too affected by the rain; it was quite firm. We hammered the pegs in and made a fair job of putting up a tent that, hurricanes excluded, should stand up for the night.

'I hope you've got *two* sleeping bags, Mr. Bond!'

'Of coursh, Mish Moneypenny!' I replied, affecting Sean Connery's accent. 'Actually, it's more like we're the other way round. After all, you're the spy! Anyway, you know I have. You had a good look through the stuff before we set off.'

'OK, OK, I was just…'

'Making a point.'

'Yeah.'

We crawled inside the tent and, slipping off our coats and jumpers, we wrestled our way into the sleeping bags and zipped them up.

I couldn't believe I was sharing a tent with a real. Live. Girl! Sleeping barely a foot away from her. To cover up my embarrassment, I plucked up my courage and decided to tell a joke.

'I know a joke about camping, do you want to hear it?'

'I'm sure you want to tell me. Go on!'

'Well, Sherlock Holmes and Dr Watson are on a camping tour of Switzerland, right?'

'Right. Is this before the Reichenbach Falls?'

'Do you mind if I tell this?'

'No, sorry, go on.'

'Well. They're lying there under the stars and Holmes turns to Watson and says: 'Look up, Watson, what do you see?'

And Watson says, 'Why, the night sky Holmes, the night sky with myriads of stars filling the heavens with their gentle light.'

'And what does that tell you, Watson?'

'Well, it tells me that we all have our place in the universe, that God's creation is beautiful, and that all is right with the world... What does it tell you Holmes?'

'It tells me that someone has stolen our blasted tent!'

There was a pause, then a chuckle, then a giggle, then a guffaw. Soon she was laughing fit to burst, I could feel the tent shaking.

'Hey, it wasn't *that* funny.'

It was a moment before she could speak. She wiped tears of laughter from her eyes and sat up in her sleeping bag. She resembled a sort of adorable Alice-in-Wonderland caterpillar, with a girl's face. She looked down at me.

'Not bad, Phil-Will, not bad. You know, I've never met a boy like you. Any other guy I know would have sworn at sleeping in a tent. You really don't swear, do you?'

I winced. 'No. I never really have liked swearing, don't know why.'

She leaned over and kissed me on the nose. 'Night night, comedy-boy.' She carried on chuckling as she settled down.

We fell asleep.

— CHAPTER THIRTEEN —
Agent Plus One Going North

It had been an emotional and tiring day, and I slept better than I would have thought. I awoke to the sun blazing through the wall of the tent.

'It wasn't a dream then?' said a voice next to me. It always takes me a while to wake up, but Elise was alert the second her eyes opened. 'Come on,' she said, 'let's get going. We'll find somewhere to have breakfast on the way.'

'Mmm?' I mumbled.

'I really, really hope this Snake Inn has a bath and towels when we get there. I stink.' She leaned over me. 'You stink too!'

'Mmm?'

She unzipped my sleeping bag and rolled me over. 'Wakey, wakey sleepyhead. Oh-oh, I need to pee, I hope there's not a queue. You men have it so easy!'

I crawled out of the wreckage of my night's sleep, and out of the carnage she had created of my bedding. She undid the ties of the tent flap and disappeared into the early morning light.

I began to come round. How could she be so lively so early in the morning? I yawned, stretched, and tried to snap out of it. I began, sleepily, to fold everything up, ready to put in the car. Then I realised I needed the toilet as well. On my way out, I met her on the way back.

'Can't stop,' I gasped as I hurried to the toilet block. She giggled and went on her way.

After I had been to the toilet and had a bit of a wash, I joined her at the tent. She had already finished packing everything up. The tent was neatly folded and back in its bag, the sleeping bags were tightly rolled, and tied with string.

'You don't waste time, do you?'

'Nope! Come on, it's already seven o'clock. Let's get on the road and find some breakfast.'

We packed up the car in two minutes flat, by simply throwing everything onto the back seats. We jumped in. I was ready for her this time and I was in my seat with the door almost closed, as we shot away from the parking spot.

'Where to, navigator?'

'Er, back the way we came, we're almost going back to Dokesley,' I racked my brain trying to remember, as I got the map out of the door pocket, 'The A38. Again.'

We had a brief stop for breakfast and taking turns to drive we made it back to the roundabout where five roads meet by one thirty in the afternoon. There was a brand-new Little Chef restaurant near the roundabout. Motoring was gradually becoming a wider pastime in the 1960s, as cars became cheap enough for more people to have one. The owners of Little Chef cashed in on this by building restaurants along the A roads. They served good basic food in a clean café, fit for families, much nicer than the greasy spoons. We stopped for lunch, and Elise filled the car with petrol at the garage next door, while I ordered fish and chips for both of us. The food was ready and waiting on her return.

'How much further, navigator?' she asked with her mouth full.

'Not too bad, now. We take the A57 to Sheffield and out the other side. The Snake Pass is part of the A57. Another hour should do it. Maybe less the way you drive!'

'Or maybe two if you drive!'

'Yeah, but at least we'd get there in one piece!' I retorted. 'You don't know the Snake Pass. It's all steep hills and sharp bends. You need to be careful.'

'OK.' She handed me the keys. 'Your turn, old slow-but-sure.'

'What?' I gulped. My bluff had been called. I had never actually driven along the Snake. I was terrified at the prospect, but I couldn't back out now.

'OK,' I said weakly.

She laughed. 'That'll teach you to criticise my

driving. Seriously, if you know this road, it's best you do it.' She finished her fish and chips with every sign of pleasure, while I toyed with mine, feeling more than a bit queasy, just thinking about the Snake.

That was how I came to be negotiating the streets of Sheffield, and heading up and out of the town along the A57. Luckily there wasn't a great deal of traffic. The road climbed back and forth, through one series of perilous bends after another. We kept climbing, up through the Pennines, until we got to the head of the pass. Then down again. Then one last up. Finally, there was the inn, overlooking the Ladybower reservoir. I'd never been so relieved to arrive at a destination in my life.

The inn is on a bend and I had to judge when to turn right into the car park. It was touch-and-go. A lorry missed us by not very much as I shot across the front of it.

'Wow, way to go, Stirling Moss!' said my companion admiringly.

I gulped audibly. 'We're here!' I croaked.

'And there's the statement of the month, from the Brain of Britain!' she said pointing to the huge sign, which I had not seen, which read 'The Snake Pass Inn' in letters three feet high.

I stuck my tongue out. She did the same and laughed. 'Let's go, Stirling!' she said, and we went into the inn. She made my heart skip a beat when she took my arm and leaned over towards me. Unfortunately, it was not for a kiss but for a hiss, in my ear.

'Listen, the cover story, right? We are brother and sister, OK? I'm Jenny Williams and you can be your sweet self. Now for the story. What are we doing here, navigator?' I racked my brains for a sensible answer.

'OK,' I managed to reply, finally. 'We are going to spend a few days here to explore the local area. It's quite picturesque. Kinder Scout's not far away, and Mam Tor, and there's Chatsworth House…' It was after four o'clock in the afternoon by now, and the sun was high in the sky. It had turned out to be a hot day. The countryside, shimmering in the heat, was looking its best. The view looking out from the inn across the Derwent valley, was stunning.

'Whoa, OK. More information than I needed right now.'

'Well they might ask what we want to see.'

'Yeah? Well you can answer, travel-guide boy.'

'Listen, Elise. Erm, how are you off for money? Because, I'm kind of broke and you keep paying for everything.'

She pulled her purse out of her pocket and took a card from it 'American Express!' she remarked, flourishing the card. 'Never leave home without it,' she added, quoting the adverts.

My knowledge of financial matters was as great as my knowledge of the far side of the moon. Nobody I knew had credit cards; in fact, they were very rare in those days. American Express was, and is, a charge card, which is slightly different thing to a credit card.

'What exactly does it do?' I asked.

She stared at me for a moment.

'This is not the time for a lesson in economics!' she exclaimed and sighed. 'All right look, it's a magic card that allows me to pay for stuff without using money, and the service picks up the bill, OK?'

'OK.' I was impressed. It really did seem like magic to me. I had seen the signs 'American Express accepted' and the slogan 'don't leave home without them', etc., in shops and garages; usually in posh places, without ever really knowing what it meant.

We walked towards the inn, and into reception. As we went, I tried to work it out. I was aware that you could have an account at a store, or a garage and pay it off at the end of the month.

'So, it's like having an account at a shop, only this is accepted at lots of shops, and you pay it off at the end of the month or something?'

'Give the boy a carrot!'

I shook my head. I still couldn't get my head round it altogether. How did they know who you were?

We went into the reception area of the inn. Elise went up to the counter. There was a smartly dressed young woman behind it.

'How can I help?' she asked, in broad Sheffield.

'Hi, my brother and I would like two single rooms, please…' Elise replied in elegant posh.

The woman looked around. 'Where's your luggage?' she inquired in her forthright Yorkshire manner. I held up my rucksack.

Elise looked at me. 'Oh, oops, mine's in the car, we'll get it later,' she ended. I wasn't sure the woman believed her. She looked at us appraisingly. From the doubtful expression on her face, I guessed she was trying to work out who or what we were. In the end I suppose she accepted that it was none of her business. She shook her head, she pulled herself together, and she got back to her task.

'Could you fill in these forms please?' she said briskly. She turned to me. 'That will be nine guineas for the week, sir, in advance.'

Elise broke in. '*I'm* paying. You take American Express, don't you? Right, here's the card. Phil you do the forms. Fill the forms, Phil. Ha-ha, get it?'

The American Express card worked its magic, and the woman became instantly more respectful. I dutifully put my name and address, then added my 'sister' Jenny Williams at the same address. Elise looked at the forms as the woman behind the counter busied herself with the American Express card. Elise gave me her approval. She smiled at me and nodded.

The woman was giving us the lowdown on the hotel, as Elise signed the payment slip:

'Breakfast is from seven until nine, no latecomers will be served,' she said in the sing-song way of someone reciting a lesson learned by heart. 'There are two bathrooms on every floor. We serve meals in the restaurant from seven o'clock. It's à la carte. Breakfast is included in the price, but other meals are extra. You pay for everything at the end of your stay.' She took a deep breath after this recitation and smiled at us. 'Now, is there anything else I can help you with?'

Elise spoke up, 'Er, yes, actually. We're er, we're touring round the country. Mother was going to send us some things, letters from home and so on. She has this joke where she calls us daft code names! A-ha-ha! Erm, do you have anything for Sigma One?'

'Oh wait, there was something, I couldn't work out what it was all about. Here it is!' She bent down and produced a large envelope filled with papers, from a shelf under the counter. It had the address of the inn on it, and 'to be collected, under the name of Sigma One' written in large letters across it. 'It came by special messenger.'

She flourished it with the air of a conjuror showing off his best trick. Elise grabbed it, turned away, then remembered her manners. She turned back.

'Thanks, thanks very much,' she jabbered, before heading off at speed.

'Don't you want your keys?' The woman called after her rapidly disappearing form.

Elise came back somewhat red-faced.

'Er, thanks.'

'Room sixteen and seventeen on the first floor.'

I thanked the woman and rolled my eyes as if to indicate 'sisters, eh?' I scampered after Elise who was already halfway up the stairs with the precious envelope.

— CHAPTER FOURTEEN —
Agent Found

She took the key to room sixteen and went in. It was a nice room, comparatively spacious, in fact. There was the single bed, a dressing table and stool, a small sofa, and an armchair. A big step up from the boarding house we had been in the day before. I went into room seventeen, to dump my things. I put my jacket on a chair, and my rucksack in the wardrobe, and I returned to room sixteen. I joined Elise on the sofa as she was riffling through the papers.

'There are details here of all the missions of the babies,' she said. 'There were five of us left after a couple of people dropped out. They couldn't take the training.' She said it casually enough, but once more there was unmistakable pride in her voice.

'But *you* could, and you completed your mission. The only one who did!' I enthused.

'With your help!'

'Even so.'

She smiled. 'Yeah, I did, didn't I?' Oh, what that

smile did to me! A kind of goofiness came over me.

'Elise is a lovely name,' I blurted. She looked up from the papers she was examining.

'Thank you. It means pledged to God. Mum said it was because my dad couldn't spell. He was supposed to call me after one of my aunts, Elsie, but he got it wrong on the register of my birth! Elsie means noble, I'd have preferred that.' We both laughed.

She turned back to the papers.

'Look, here's the schedule for the missions of the babies. They were all over the place. One was in Scotland, one in Wales, one in Dover, and one in London, and I got the bloody north Midlands. There are addresses and telephone numbers here for the hotels and boarding houses they were staying in.' She pulled a wry smile. 'None of them are what you would call five-star establishments. My hotel in Bramley was probably the best of the lot. It had two stars.'

There was also a short, typed list of addresses, headed 'safe houses'. Some had been crossed off the list. Someone had added the word 'still' in pen to the heading, so that it now read 'still safe houses'. There were four left, four deemed to be still safe. There was a set of four Yale keys in the envelope.

'Good to know they're "still" safe,' said Elise. 'You know, I'd feel happier with these papers locked in the car boot. Would you mind, Phil? I don't think the inn is all that secure.' She kept the sheet with the information about the places the other four trainees had been staying in. The sheet had the phone numbers, too, which meant she could try and contact them.

I went down to the car with the remaining wad of papers and locked it in the boot. I had a brainwave. To create the illusion that Elise had some luggage, I brought up the sleeping bags and tent, roughly bundled up in my coat. I smiled at the woman behind the counter, as I struggled towards the stairs with this unwieldy package.

'Her luggage!' I exclaimed. She gave me a wan smile. I wrestled my way upstairs with this awkward load and dumped it on the floor in my room; then went back to Elise.

When I got there, she was in the middle of making phone calls. She had phoned each establishment on the list in turn and got the same answer at each of them. There had been no sign of Mr Green, Mr Brown, or Mr Black for some days, according to their respective landladies. Finally, she phoned the Scottish number. At last she got an answer.

'Mr Gray?' she asked. The professional mask slipped briefly. 'Oh, Jack, it's so good to hear your voice,' she babbled. 'Ahem.' She regained her professional demeanour. 'It's Miss White here, Mr Gray.'

Miss White eh? She hadn't told me that, I thought.

She continued, 'This is not a secure line. I have bad news. The manager of the firm is away, and I am deputising for him. I have been given his title and I am trying to save what's left of the firm.'

I went over and she held the phone so I could listen.

'You're now Sigma One?'

'That's affirmative, Mr Gray. I need you to leave there immediately, repeat immediately. The security of the firm has been breached, and I have been unable to contact any other members of the team. Don't wait for anything, put the phone down now and go, go quickly. Meet me at the Snake Inn on the A57 in Derbyshire as soon as you can. Room sixteen. Is that understood?'

'Er yes, Miss White, understood.' He paused for thought, as if calculating routes and timings. 'I'll be there early tomorrow, I'm leaving now.'

Elise put the phone down.

'Well, that's that. All we can do now is wait for Jack to get here. Then we'll all put our heads together and see what to do next.'

'OK,' I said.

She must have detected what P.G. Wodehouse would have called 'a rummy something' in my voice.

'What's wrong?'

'Nothing.'

'Come on, out with it.'

'I'm being silly.'

'Well, I guessed that, but tell me anyway.'

'I got used to it being just the two of us.' I pouted.

'Oh, what a face,' she teased. 'Look when this is all over, we'll have a proper holiday, OK? Just you and me.'

I was taken completely aback. 'You really mean that?'

'Yes. Of course. Silly Philly-Willy!' She came over and gave me a kiss on the cheek, and a hug.

I was back on cloud nine. I had to speak my mind, however. I did so, hesitantly, 'Elise, erm, do you remember what that lady said?'

'Which lady?'

'The one on the phone, you know, "whirlwind" and all that.'

'Oh, yes, what in particular?'

'About not trusting anybody.'

'Not trusting… You mean… Jack? Mr Gray?' She laughed. 'He's lovely. Lovely, but not that bright. He's not got the brains to think up a plot like this.'

'OK, but maybe don't tell him about me, not just yet.'

'All right, if you say so. But why? Three heads are better than two.'

I searched my head for some reasonable excuse. 'Erm, well, I, I can be your secret weapon.'

She put her head on one side. 'Look, I trust Jack as much as I trust you.' She was tired, and she was getting irritable. 'But if you want to play games, then fine.' She had not been cross with me before; sarcastic, playful, scornful at times, but not cross. It was unbearable.

'Better safe than sorry,' was all I could say. I was in a sulk, and I couldn't hide it.

'Fine.'

'Fine!'

I went back to my room to carry on sulking. She stayed in hers. I was upset because she was annoyed with me, I was annoyed with myself for being jealous – and showing it – but at the same time, deep down, I was genuinely concerned. How come this one youth was the only member of the group to survive; apart from Elise, who was quite naturally special in my eyes? I mean, I knew *her* story, but what was his? I kept returning in my mind to the phrase: 'trust no one, repeat, no one.'

Or was it really just jealousy on my part? I had had her all to myself for the last two days, and it had been joyous. By now, I had to admit to myself that I was ocean-deep in love with her. Now there was to be a third person present, someone she worked and trained with, shared triumphs and failures with. Love, jealousy and petulance were unfamiliar emotions to me. I sat and stewed in this emotional broth for some time.

I was to learn that Elise never stayed mad for long. The old cliché about people with red hair seemed to be true in her case. She flared up quickly and cooled down just as quickly.

There was a knock on my door.

'Are you finished sulking now?' came her voice through my door. 'Because I'd like to go and get something to eat.'

I was so relieved she was still talking to me. I threw

open the door and gave her a big hug. She hesitated for a moment, before responding. She hugged me back. She pulled away and looked at me.

'Well, that was unexpected. Nice, but unexpected. I guess you *are* over your sulk then?'

'Yes,' I said,' I told you I was being silly. After this is all over, we'll have a holiday like you said.'

'Good, but I've had a think, too. I won't say anything about you if you don't want me to. I've largely kept you out of it, so far, anyway. It's become a habit.'

So that was settled. For some reason I couldn't explain, I was very relieved. We went down to see what delights the restaurant of the Snake Inn offered. There was a small menu, but it was nice enough. As a starter, prawn cocktail was considered the height of sophistication in my circle. So, I had that and followed it with sirloin steak and black forest gateau to finish. Very nice. I had my first wine. We shared a bottle. Up to then I had been a half of lager-and-lime man. Tough guy, eh? The wine eased things, and we were soon complete friends again.

We went up to bed after the meal, laughing and joking.

'I'll see you in the morning, if you don't burst after all that food,' she teased.

'Ha, what about you! Half a chicken, followed by those profiterole things.'

She looked at me. 'I like you, Phil-Will,' she said,

and she *actually* kissed me on the *actual* lips.

'I like you too, Elsie,' I replied, and we kissed again. She broke gently away. 'Goodnight, Phil.'

'G-Goodnight… D-Damn!' I heard her silvery laugh as she closed the door.

— CHAPTER FIFTEEN —
Agent Down

It had been a long day with a lot of driving, and a fair amount of wine. I climbed into bed and fell asleep straight away. At around about half past two in the morning, however, I was awakened by my hair-trigger hearing. The wine had left my mouth dry, my head aching and my brain foggy, but my ears were as sharp as ever. Sleepily, I tried to identify what it was that had disturbed me. There were noises, noises I couldn't identify. It took me a while to focus on them and locate the source. They were coming from next door, from Elise's room.

I stumbled out of bed and listened carefully. There were whispers; I couldn't make out what was being said, but a dagger of jealousy stabbed me in the heart. Had Jack arrived early? Was I being left out while they made plans and talked spy talk? Adrenalin surged through me, and the mists in my brain cleared, like fog before a strong wind. I was wide awake now, and I was, unreasonably, angry.

I listened again. This time, I heard something much more disturbing. There were sounds as if someone was trying to speak, but the someone was being muffled with a hand or something over their mouth. I was in my new habit of sleeping in my underwear. I was in no fit state to leave the room. I grabbed my clothes and pulled them on as quickly as I could go. It sounded like Elise was in trouble. I heard her door open, and I paused with my trousers half on, and I pressed my ear against my door.

Whoever it was, was deliberately making as little noise as they could. There were no more muffled speech sounds. They must have quietened Elise in some way. Was she even still alive? Oh God; that thought nearly had me rushing out, there and then, one leg in and one leg out of my trousers! Fortunately, I took a deep breath. I pulled on trousers and jumper. It gave me a second for reflection. I paused, to try and learn more. Continuing small sounds, the creak of a stair, a whispered oath, told me that they, whoever 'they' were, were moving away, down the stairs.

What would the Saint do? He'd use his head, that's what. He'd be subtle. I waited a moment longer, and then cautiously poked my head out of the door. No one in sight. I went into Elise's room. My heart lurched in my chest. She was no longer there. Her bed was empty, and the bedclothes were all on the floor in a heap.

The rooms on this side of the hotel not only had a

great view of the countryside, they also had a great view of the car park. I heard a car start. I rushed over to the window in time to see it pull away. I didn't think once, let alone twice, I reacted instinctively. The girl I adored was in trouble, and I was going after her. I searched frantically for Elise's car keys, and I found them in a drawer of the little cupboard by the bed. Something else was also in the drawer, something which I thought might come in handy. I pocketed it and raced downstairs.

I ran into the car park and jumped into the Mini. I was a seasoned driver by now. I made a racing start that would have made Jackie Stewart proud. I sped off in the direction the other car had taken. Whatever state she was in, Elise was in that car, and I wasn't going to abandon her.

The souped-up Mini showed its paces as I raced along the road, headlights on full beam, desperate to catch a glimpse of their taillights. We were heading back towards Sheffield. At that time of the morning there were no other cars on the road. If I saw a taillight, it had to be them. I drove like a man possessed. The Mini clung to the road like the superb rally car it was.

At last I saw lights on the road before me. They were below and about half a mile ahead. I saw their headlights on full beam as they negotiated a series of hairpin bends. How many times I nearly went over the side as I raced after them, I wouldn't care to contemplate. One false move, and I would have been hurtling over the edge of the steep fells to my death. I think it helped with it being dark. What I couldn't see, I didn't worry about. That's not to say my heart wasn't in my mouth every yard of that road, it was but I was more frantic about Elise than I was about the road. I drove on at a reckless pace.

At last I came up behind them. I would give myself away, if I followed them too closely. As agitated as I was, I had the presence of mind to pull back. In the pitch-black night, I could see them quite well even from a distance. They were driving the only car on the road, and their full-beam headlights lit up the countryside for all to see for miles around. I followed them all the way back into Sheffield.

At last we had left the perilous Snake pass behind. I vowed that if at all possible, Elise was going to do the driving on the way back. I never wanted to do that run again. Twice in one day was too much, especially since one of the journeys was done at high speed, and in the dark!

I was drenched in sweat and the tension was making my whole body ache. We drove through Sheffield. I began to think we were heading back to Dokesley, but while we were still in the city, they turned off the main road, and into some side streets.

They drove into a quiet residential road on the further edge of Sheffield and parked up. It was a short cul-de-sac of small terraced houses. I stopped the car briefly at the entrance to the street. I was burning to know what had happened to Elise. I wanted to dash to her rescue, but something held me back. Some would say it was cowardice, but I prefer to think it was common sense.

On the one hand there were at least two tough, army-trained, battle-hardened men, probably with guns, and on the other hand there was – well, let's face it – skinny, cowardly peaceable me. What was I going to do, talk them to sleep?

Enough said! In spite of my desperation about the girl I was deeply in love with, I was able to muster enough sense to drive on past the end of the cul-de-sac, so that I could stop somewhere to think. I parked on the main road – there were far fewer double yellow lines in those days – and ran back to the cul-de-sac. I peeped around the corner at the top of the little street. I was in time to see two men lifting a girl-shaped, sheet-swathed bundle out of the saloon car. Being a car nerd, I noted the brand. It was an Austin Princess 1300, a popular car of the time. I approved their choice, it would blend in. Not like a Rolls or a Jag – or a Mini Cooper.

They carried their burden into a house. They moved swiftly and quietly. I didn't have much time. I needed a plan, and fast. If Elise was still alive, they would be trying to get information out of her. I had seen enough spy films to know that, when guys like this wanted information quickly, they weren't gentle. There was already a light on in the house before they went in, showing that there was probably someone else already in there. I noted the house and remembered its position. At that time of the morning, it was the only one lit up in the whole street.

When they had gone inside, I did a quick recce on foot. I examined the area both in front, and behind, the houses. These were terraced houses, but there was a little passage at the back, leading off the main road, so that the dustbin collectors could do their work. I crept down this passage and located the back of the right house by means of careful counting. The garden gate was locked, but it was easy enough to climb over, even for me. I tried to do it as quietly as possible. I winced as my shoes scraped noisily on the wooden gate as I scrambled up and over. I managed it in the end – without quite waking up the whole of Sheffield. I crouched down in the garden on the other side and wiped sweat from my face. The back of the house was in darkness.

OK, Phil-Will, now what? I thought. The garden was barely visible in the dim glow from distant streetlights. It was not well-kept. It was mostly bare soil, populated with a few hardy tufts of grass clinging on for dear life, along with dandelions and other weeds. Some wood was stacked next to a little shed. I picked up one of the pieces of wood, and I swung it experimentally. It was solid, and heavy. It could do some damage, if it was used properly. The snag was, I had no idea how to use it properly – or at all. I had never used a weapon, of any sort, in my whole life. On the telly people clonked the villain on the head, and he immediately fell unconscious. Did that happen in real life? I didn't know. I didn't want to kill anyone; nor did I want to hit them too gently and leave them conscious and fighting mad.

'Philip Williams, what are you doing you great idiot?' I asked myself. Unfortunately, myself replied, 'Elise is in trouble, now shut up and get going!'

I clung tightly onto the piece of wood as though I was drowning, and it was a lifebelt. I reconnoitred the place, looking for a way in. There was a coal-shed – a little outhouse with a sloping roof – against the back of the house. It reached up almost to the first-floor windows. These were in the standard pattern of the time. Two larger single-glazed windows, fastened with a catch, two smaller windows at the top. One of the little windows was slightly open.

Still trying to hang on to that wretched lump of two by four, I scrambled onto the shed. I balanced perilously on the sloping roof on tiptoe. In this precarious position, clinging to the window ledge, I could just about manage to peep through the window. There were no curtains, it was very dim inside, but the room seemed deserted. Encouraged, I reached up. My fingers were tantalisingly close to the partially open window. I put the lump of wood down and stood on it, gaining an extra four inches. It was just about enough. I walked my fingers up to the open window.

I grasped the edge of the frame with my fingertips, steadied myself, then got a foot onto the sill. I heaved myself up, straining arms legs and fingers – and the window frame – until I was standing upright on the perilously narrow window-ledge, clutching on and swaying like a spider in a gale.

I put my arm through the small window and released the catch on the bigger window below. I forgot where I was standing. I nearly swept myself off the ledge as the larger window swung open. I hung precariously for a moment, dangling by one arm and one leg. I recovered my balance and clambered inside, shutting the window behind me.

If all the 'reds' in England were under the bed at that moment, I couldn't go on. I had to rest. I was shaking from the exertion and the nervous tension. My legs went from under me, and I sat down heavily on a small divan bed. It was only then that I realised I had sacrificed my weapon in order to reach the open window. I couldn't go back for it now. I remember thinking, *weaponless in the house of the enemy.*

The room was lit only by the faintest illumination from the remote streetlights, filtering through the grimy glass. After I had got my breath back, and when my legs would support me once more, I made my way to the door. It was only visible because it didn't fit properly into its frame, and the light from the landing gave it an outline. I put my ear to the door. I heard nothing.

My ideas on torturing people for information were very much gleaned from the films I'd seen. I expected to hear screams; perhaps, evil laughter. But there was nothing.

I opened the door a crack and peeped out. Silence. Nothing to be seen or heard. The bulb on the landing was dim but compared with the light inside the room, it was dazzling. I took a precious moment to let my eyes adjust. The floor was lino again, noisier than carpet, I had to step very carefully. All those times my dad had worked nights came in handy. As careful as I was, my shoes went 'week' with every step on the shiny floor. With every limb trembling, expecting to be caught any second, I sneaked – and squeaked – towards the top of the stairs. Now, I could hear something: a murmur of voices, coming from downstairs. I froze. After a moment, I realised that they weren't speaking English. I assumed it was Russian. It was all Greek to me!

It didn't sound like torture, or even tough questioning, it sounded like people chatting. An idea began to form in my mind. If they weren't interrogating Elise down there, she must be somewhere else. Maybe she was up here, lying somewhere, unconscious... or even dead? That dreadful thought galvanised me and gave me the courage to go on. I started to breathe again. I decided to explore further. I crossed the landing, I looked through the open bathroom door, no-one there. I approached the door to another bedroom as quietly as I could. I tried the door. It was locked. *Aha!* I thought. The key was in the lock. I took hold of it. What was I going to find inside that locked room? I swallowed hard and forced myself on.

The key was stiff, my heart was in my mouth as it creaked round. It unlocked with a loud click. My nerves were strung to such a pitch that, to my ears, it sounded like a pistol shot. I waited, holding my breath, no reaction from downstairs. I could still hear the quiet murmur of voices. I let my breath out and opened the door. I crept into the darkened room.

I had just paused for a second, to try and adjust my eyes once again to the darkness of the room, when all hell broke loose. Someone grabbed me by the arm and threw me down to the floor. I landed with a crash and bashed my head, badly, against the wall. The room swam around me, my head really hurt, and I felt sick. In the dim light, and with spinning head, I could just make out a lamp raised on high ready to bash me – forcefully. I winced, raised my arms and waited for the blow. This was really going to hurt! I waited; I waited some more, then there was someone's body on top of me, weighing me down. A hand was placed over my mouth and a voice hissed in my ear,

'Oh God, I'm sorry, I'm so sorry, Phil-Will. I thought it was one of them! Are you all right? Say you're all right!'

— CHAPTER SIXTEEN —
Agent at Work

It was Elise, of course, fully conscious and fighting mad. My head was still swimming. She took her hand from my mouth. I needed a few more seconds to recover before I could speak. In the interval, she used the lamp for its proper purpose. She set it up right again and switched it on so that we could at least see each other.

'Phil! Phil-Will, are you all right?' she repeated in a loud whisper. The sight of her pretty face, wracked with anxiety over me, was like balm to my soul.

After a further agonised moment or two, I found my voice. 'We've got to stop meeting secretly in bedrooms,' I groaned, quietly. Pretty good, I thought in the circumstances!

'Oh, I don't know... it could be worse,' she said with a relieved smile and a raised eyebrow.

'Are you all right, not hurt?' I asked, lying as still as I could, while waves of nausea swept over me.

She got off me. 'Only my pride. I fought them, but

they took me by surprise when I was asleep. I didn't stand a chance. They bundled me up in the bedclothes. I tried to shout out to you, but they had a hand over my mouth. One of them injected me with something, and I lost consciousness. When I came round, I was here. They looked in on me a little while ago, but I played possum. I thought you were them, coming back to check on me again.' She gave me a warm smile. My heart melted, and my pain faded a little.

'But how did you get here?' she asked. 'It's like a miracle.'

'Something woke me, maybe you, shouting my name. I heard them in your room. When they drove off, I followed them, in the Mini.'

'Attaboy!' She became business-like. She helped me to my feet. 'I take it you have our escape route worked out, plan boy?'

I hadn't of course, I was making it up as I went along, but I didn't tell her that!

'Come on,' I whispered. I led the way back across the landing and into the dark room on the other side. My head ached, and I was still dizzy from the blow against the wall, but time was short, and I forced myself to keep going.

'Wait,' she whispered, before she nipped back across the landing, relocked the door of her former prison and pocketed the key. 'That will give them something to think about!' She flashed me a mischievous smile. 'And it might buy us some time.'

We slipped back into the first room and I opened the window.

'You'll have to drop on to that coal-shed roof,' I whispered. 'Be careful. It slopes quite steeply.'

She nodded her understanding. She lowered herself carefully down and landed on the sloping roof lightly, like a mountain chamois. She then dropped gracefully to the ground. I lowered myself down, lost my footing on the sloping roof and fell like a sack of potatoes, with a crash. Embarrassed and in pain I leapt to my feet, helped by her strong right arm.

'Quick,' I panted, 'this way.' We ran – or rather she ran and I hobbled – to the back gate where, greatly to my surprise, she dropped onto her hands and knees. She indicated for me to stand on her back so that I could scramble painfully over. Once I was over, she sprang for the top of the fence and nimbly dropped down.

'Don't think I'm going to make a habit of going down on my hands and knees for you!' she joked, as she brushed herself down.

I didn't get the joke. 'Of course not,' I replied with all seriousness.

She gave me that wry smile I had seen before; she shook her head and sighed. 'Where's the car?'

We went out of the little back alley, and out onto the main road.

She grabbed my hand, I was thrilled. My heart was singing as we ran back to the car hand-in-hand. We jumped in. She got into the driver's seat. I was only too pleased to let her drive. Apart from the fact that I was still shaking from the adrenalin rush, my head was still spinning from its collision with the wall. I didn't fancy that drive back along the snake, and I said so.

'We can't go back, we're blown! There will be at least one opposition team swarming all over the place by now,' she explained.

'But what about all my stuff, my camping gear?'

'Your camping gear? Oh, you mean that antediluvian tent, and those 1940's sleeping bags? Don't worry Phil-Will, I'll buy you some more, some nice new stuff. Luckily, I keep my purse and things in my pocket. I learned the habit from you boys. It's harder to fight with a handbag in your hand! I decided to sleep in my clothes, too, in case Mr Gray turned up.' She grinned at me. Then her face became serious, 'I'm sorry, Phil, but we really can't go back to the inn.'

I opened my mouth, twice, to say something and twice I thought better of it.

She saw me. 'Something you want to say country boy?'

I shook my head. 'No, no. Not a thing!'

'Good!'

There was no need to emphasise the point. It was clear 'Mr Gray' had betrayed her, us.

'You know, I still can't see you with a handbag!' I teased.

She laughed, put the Mini into gear and drove off;

then to my surprise, she stopped almost immediately. She had pulled into the alley right opposite the street the crooks were in. She turned the car round, so it was facing back towards the main road, and parked up behind a Hillman Hunter. She could see their cul-de-sac, but a casual glance in this direction would not spot the mini hidden behind the other car.

'Get some rest, Phil-Will. We might be here for a little while.'

I was bewildered. I felt sure she would want to put as many miles between us and them as possible. I said so.

'Listen,' she said in the manner of someone giving a lecture, 'there may be clues in that house. We have to get in there to get a look around, but not until they've gone. I'll take first watch; I've had more sleep than you.'

She put down the back of the Mini's passenger seat for me and fussed over me a bit; it was nice. She made me close my eyes, in a motherly fashion. I lay back. It seemed like a few seconds later that she nudged me.

'They just pulled out and shot off, going like a bat out of hell, heading back towards the Snake. They'll get caught speeding if they're not careful. Come on, sleepy head, you've had an hour; what more do you want? The game's afoot, Watson!'

I groaned. 'Thought we were doing Bond and Moneypenny?'

'Actually, I kind of see you more as some kind of

behind the scenes boffin.'

'"Q" you mean? That's nice.' I yawned.

'Come *on*, Phil.' She got out of the car. I followed her trying to wake up.

'I should never have had that wine,' I grumbled.

She giggled. 'Two glasses?'

I replied indignantly, 'They were big glasses!'

That made her laugh again. Still chuckling, she led the way back to the house in the cul-de-sac. 'How many of them did you see? Remember to divide by two, since you were drunk!'

I drew myself up and replied, as haughtily as I could, 'There were two of them. First at the Inn, when they were carrying you into the car, then into that house. They were all muffled up with their hats pulled down low, I didn't get a good look at them.'

'Never mind. Be careful,' she murmured quietly, 'they will have left someone on guard. They usually work in threes.' I nodded. There had been three in Dokesley on both previous occasions we had met them. These might even be the same three.

We paused at the top of the street. She crouched down behind a post-box. I crouched with her. She seemed to be deciding on the next move. I was still trying to shake off my nausea and my dizziness, but I was bubbling over with happiness. After fearing the worst, Elise beaten up or even dead, I felt really happy that she was all right. And I had rescued her. Me! I felt triumphant. I was in a flippant mood. 'We could try something really subtle like ringing the doorbell,' I joked.

'Hmm, not bad. My type of approach. OK, let's do it.' She began to get up.

'I was kidding!'

But it was too late. She was off. She marched boldly up to the front door and rang the bell.

I raced after her. 'Shame we haven't got that gun,' she said conversationally.

'But I do have the gun,' I said. I had picked it up when I got Elise's car keys. Not that I would have known how to use it.

'Quick give it to me,' she hissed as footsteps approached the door. 'Get out of sight! And stay out of sight, until I come for you.'

'But…' I protested. She just gave me a look. It was the kind of look that your worst nightmare of a teacher would give when you told her you hadn't done your homework. I retreated hastily.

She cocked the gun and put it back in her pocket.

The man opened the door. Peeping out from my hiding place I recognised one of the men that had been waiting by her car back in Dokesley. It seemed like it was an age ago, but it had only been two days. He had a bottle of beer in his hand as he opened the door; in his other hand a cigarette dangled.

'Вы быстро вернулись. Ты забирала ее?' he said as he was opening the door, clearly believing that his comrades had come back.

He had on vest and trousers, with braces dangling down. He was in his stockinged feet.

When he saw who was at the door, he stared, astonished, at the girl who had been his captive only an hour or so ago. Elise gave him a crooked smile, then she stepped back out of arms' reach and brought the gun up to the level of his chest. '*Руки вверх!*' It sounded like 'perruque-yum viveer'. The startled man clearly understood. He took one look at Elise's stony face, then a second look at the gun. He did as he was told and put up his hands.

'*Иди в дом и сядь,*'she snapped. The man obeyed. He went into the house and sat down in the living room. I peeped through the window, where there was a gap in the curtains. Elise kept the gun on him, while with her other hand she reached for the man's shirt, which he had put over a chair. She threw it to him.

'*повязку себя,*'she said. He wrapped the shirt round his head and tied the sleeves at the back. He was now blindfolded. Elise checked. She aimed a blow at him with the butt of the gun. I winced, I thought she was really going to hit him, but she stopped just one inch short. He didn't flinch. The blindfold was obviously effective. Elise gave a satisfied nod. She put away her gun. She grabbed a lamp from the sideboard in the room and tore out the flex. She tied up his hands and feet. She wasn't gentle. She trussed him up like an oven ready turkey and pushed him over, so that he was lying helpless on the settee. I felt privileged, and somewhat awed, to witness this sight of Elise in full agent mode.

She came out to get me and put her finger to her lips. I tip-toed into the room.

'Hey! *Я не могу дышать.* I can't breathe!' came a plaintive voice from the settee in a mixture of Russian and English.

'*Если вы можете говорить вы можете дышать!* If you can talk, you can breathe.' This was an Elise I had not seen before. A ruthless, cold, professional Elise.

She pointed to a chair, with her finger to her lips. I sat down as quietly as I could. I would not have dared to disobey. She was formidable in this mood. I breathed as quietly as I could. She made a thorough search of the room. She harvested a number of papers and files, which she gave to me to hold.

She went into the kitchen and picked up a sharp knife from the sink. As she approached the captive Russian, I wondered what dreadful thing she was going to do to the helpless man. She took hold of the material of the shirt, and made a small hole in it, just below his mouth.

'*Теперь вы можете дышать,*'she said. She had cut him a breathing hole.

Then we left, rapidly. It was around four o'clock in the morning.

— CHAPTER SEVENTEEN —
Safe Houses

'Don't tell me, top of the class in Russian?' I whispered, as we made for the front door.

'I had a head start,' she whispered back. 'My grandmother was Russian. She fled from persecution by the Tsar as a young woman in the late nineteenth century. She brought her family to England. My mother was born here, but grandma taught her the Russian language, and she taught me. I have "A" level Russian, but I can speak it much better than "A" level. Just don't ask me to write it!'

'So, top of the class then?' I persisted.

'OK, OK, I was top of the class in Russian. I also have a smattering of Polish and Czechoslovakian. Happy now?'

I grinned at her. 'You're amazing,' I blurted.

She blushed. 'Well, I'd better get my amazing ar...er, backside into gear. The others might come back at any moment. Come on.' She opened the door cautiously and poked her head out. There was no sign of the other men returning, so we made a run for the car.

'Where to?' I asked as we ran.

'Safe house. The list is in the boot, in that envelope, with the other stuff.' She gasped. 'You can really run, can't you? Slow down a bit!'

I went straight to the boot and grabbed the envelope and shut it with a thud. I leapt back in the car and slammed the door quickly, knowing what was about to happen. Elise put in the clutch and shot away from the kerb before I was properly down in my seat.

'Pick any of the four,' she said.

I nodded, then grabbed the door handle to save myself as she threw the Mini around the corner at the top of the little street. I found the list of four remaining safe houses, pulled it out of the documents folder and scanned it. 'The nearest one is in Doncaster,' I said. 'Back to the A1.'

She nodded, and we set off back along the A57 towards Crowton. That was a great relief to me. It had been bad enough when I was driving, but to be a passenger in the car the way Elise drives…Well, let's just say I was glad we were not going back over the Snake!

It was a quarter past four when we left Sheffield. The roads were clear. We shot back along the A57, through Crowton, and back to the roundabout where five roads meet. We turned left and headed north, up the A1.

'That roundabout is still in the parish of Dokesley,' I commented.

'Well, thank you for that amazing piece of information. You're a walking encyclopaedia, aren't you.'

I grinned. 'Welcome back, Sarky One!' I studied the map. It wasn't a difficult route to follow. The A1 went straight into Doncaster. Elise stopped at a garage for petrol, and I went into the little office and bought an A-Z map of the area. The house we wanted was on Thorne Road, near the Doncaster Infirmary.

When we arrived, I saw that it had been well chosen. It had fast access via the A60 to the A1. You could park in the street, and there was no access to the house, except from the front. On the other hand, if you needed to escape you could do so from the back of the house into the garden, and over a fence into either of the neighbours' gardens.

Daylight. Six in the morning. The bad weather of the last two weeks seemed to have worn itself out. It was looking like another bright warm day. There was a heat haze in the sky as the sun rose in shades of roses and gold.

'Let's have a bit of a sleep before we do anything else,' Elise suggested. 'I'm exhausted. Being unconscious is not the same as being asleep. Three hours, OK?'

She tried a couple of keys from the big envelope,

before finding the right one. We went in. It was not luxurious. Spartan would have been an appropriate word. At least it was clean and tidy, unlike the Russians' house. There were three bedrooms upstairs, all with camp beds, three to a room. There was a bathroom too, with a bath – hurrah! Downstairs there was the usual lounge and dining room, with a kitchen and a small utility room. This contained, amongst other things, a washing machine and a large wooden clothes horse.

No one was currently using the safe house. There were no sheets or blankets visible in the bedrooms. Elise found them in a cupboard downstairs. They were all clean and folded. We shared them between us. She took the main bedroom, and I took the one next in size. When she opened the wardrobe in her room there was real treasure in there. Dressing gowns for both of us. She gave me one.

'Take your clothes off,' she ordered. 'And before you get any ideas, I mean go back to your room and take your clothes off. All of them. Then put this on.' She handed me the larger of the two dressing gowns. 'There's a washing machine downstairs, you can put all our things in it and wash them. They'll all have to go in together. They'll come out uniform grey I bet, but at least they'll no longer stink! Then get a fire going, we'll both have a bath after we've had a sleep. Bagsy first go in the bath!'

There were no such things as showers in 1967 (in

most homes anyway), but most had baths. In many houses, especially in coal mining areas, the water was heated by a boiler at the back of the fire. This house was no exception. So, to get hot water you had to have a fire, even in the summer. There was usually enough for one, or if you were frugal with the hot water, two baths. My aunt and her weird brood, otherwise known as my cousins, would come over once a week or so. They lived in a village about six miles away. They didn't have a bathroom in their house. In addition to this, their only 'toilet' was an earth closet at the bottom of a very long garden. Ask me what the brood's father did for a living? I'll tell you. He was a builder! Talk about the cobbler's children being the worst shod! Anyway, it meant that they all came round to my hospitable mother's house to have a bath. All seven of them! They followed on from the oldest to the youngest, so I was used to sharing bathwater.

Luckily, the washing machine was very similar to our one at home. I had been obliged to work out how our machine operated when I had washed my muddy clothes a week or two before. It had taken a while to figure it out, but at least I now knew what I was doing.

I'm afraid I have no hilarious disaster stories to share with you about everything turning pink. But I was very chary about handling Elise's clothes, especially the more *personal* items, if you know what I mean. I closed my eyes, bundled everything of hers up and threw it into the machine. It was a twin tub. The 'tub' on the right washed the clothes, which then had to be transferred into the left-hand tub to be spun. There was an on button and a temperature control. That was it. Luckily, this one, unlike our machine at home, had been plumbed in, which meant I didn't have to stand and watch while it filled up. I could go up to bed, leaving the machine to do its work. I decided I would put the clothes on to spin later, after I had slept.

Before I went upstairs, I had to make and light the fire for the hot water. This was one of the few jobs I could be trusted with at home. I was good at it. The secret was to put up a sheet of newspaper across the fireplace, usually wedged in place with the coal shovel, but a couple of fire irons would do. This was to create a small draught, which would help the fire to 'draw'. It was about how you placed the wood, paper and coal as well. It was an art, one sadly lost now! There were matches in a drawer in the kitchen.

When the fire was burning merrily away, I went back upstairs. Elise's door was shut. I knocked.

'If there's a handsome prince out there, come in at once, if it's Phil…oh, come in anyway!'

'Hardy-har-har,' I said. And to quote Bertie Wooster, I meant it to sting! I entered.

'Oh, it's you,' she feigned surprise. 'I thought for a moment it was Fred Flintstone!'

It took me a second to get what she meant. 'Oh. Well, "hardy har-har" is Daffy Duck. So, there!'

'No, it's Fred Flintstone.'

'No. He says "droll, ve-ry droll",' I argued, imitating the famous cartoon caveman.

She wasn't going to back down. 'Maybe they both said it!'

I wasn't disposed to argue with her. I shrugged.

'Look at me!' She giggled, stood up from the bed and put out her arms.

I looked. The dressing gown was ludicrously big on her. The sleeves covered her hands, and the skirts of it came down to her feet and dragged on the floor.

'I look ridiculous.'

'I think you look fab.' It was true, oversized dressing gown or not, to me she did.

'You're sweet.' She smiled. 'Crazy, but sweet.' She came over and gave me a light little kiss. She kissed me on the cheek, but it made me tingle all over.

I sort of floated into the bedroom, took off my dressing gown and got into bed, just as I was. So much had changed in the last couple of weeks that sleeping without pyjamas just felt normal. As I thought of this, I smiled to myself and shook my head. I drifted off to sleep. We both slept for three hours or so. It seemed like no time at all until she was knocking on my door.

'Come on, sleeping beauty. I've had my bath and washed my hair. I left the jug in there so you can do the same.'

The fire had done its job. The bath was still fairly hot when I got into the rather grey water, she must have put up with it really very hot, so that I wouldn't have a cold bath.

I went downstairs afterwards, my skin clean and pink from the hot water. Dressed in my dressing gown, I put the washed clothes into the spin-dryer and turned it on at maximum speed. Elise was right, there was a kind of faint greyness on all the clothes when the washing machine had finished with them. I put our wet things on the large wooden clothes horse round the hearth in the living room, and stoked the fire, so that it roared up, raising clouds of steam from the drying garments. Elise came downstairs. She looked at my dressing gown.

'That fits you rather well,' she observed. 'Very dashing, very Noel Coward!' She drew up a chair and sat down by the clothes horse to dry her hair at the fire. 'Listen, I've got to stay here and translate these documents, but we can't go around all day in dressing gowns. As soon as your clothes are dry enough, can you go and buy us some clothes?'

CHAPTER EIGHTEEN

Mission Impossible

I gaped at her.

'Take the American Express card,' she continued, running her hands through her hair, and exposing it to the warmth of the fire.' My signature is easy enough to copy, no one ever looks at it anyway…'

She looked up and saw me. I was still gaping.

'What? Are you worried about the card? Don't be. It'll be fine.' I shook my head. 'What then?'

I gulped and found my voice. 'You want *me* to buy *you* clothes?'

'And some for you too. I don't know about you, but I'm fed up of smelling like the council tip!'

'B-but. *Everything*?'

Light dawned. 'Ah, this is about my underwear, isn't it?'

'I-I've never b-bought, you know, w-women's things before.'

'I bet Mummy buys all of your clothes as well, doesn't she?'

I blushed. Mummy did.

'That explains the taste! Well, now's your chance, express yourself, for God's sake! Buy some casual clothes that look nice. I'm size 10, and my bra size is 32B, inside leg…'

'B-bra size?'

She sighed. 'You can get everything in Marks and Sparks. Ask the ladies there for help if you don't know what to get. Just ordinary white cotton knickers will be fine.'

I stood beetroot red and just gawped.

'Knickers, yes. You wear them too, you know.' I was thoroughly embarrassed. She was thoroughly amused.

'I th-think you're enjoying this!' I grumbled.

'Very perceptive of you!' She giggled. 'I can't wait to see what you come back with!' She sat for a moment enjoying my discomfort, then she took pity on me. 'All right, I'll write you a list. Put the kettle on.'

She wrote a list all right, and the minx wrote it in the most embarrassing possible fashion.

Slacks, three pairs size ten –two blue, one white. INSIDE LEG 28' HIPS 33'.

BRAS THREE. SIZE 32B.

Tops, several, size: small.

Jacket, size ten.

KNICKERS WHITE. SIZE TEN, TWENTY-SIX INCH WAIST. FIVE PAIRS.

Shoes, casual, size four, two pairs.

She was wringing every last bit of amusement out of this shopping session. As she handed me the list she put on a mock-serious face and said, 'OK, double "o" three-and-a-half, don't come back without the goods. The nation is relying on you!'

'Hardy har-har,' I replied, sulkily. She laughed.

I spent the time, while we waited for the kettle to boil, in practising her signature. I wrote E. White at least twenty times, until I thought I had it.

We had coffee and something to eat from the cupboard, which was well-stocked with tins and dried food – items that would keep well. After we had eaten, I trailed out into the bright afternoon sunshine. I had the piece of paper in my pocket, and her laughter ringing in my ears. My clothes were still damp. All right they were wet, but at least clean and warm from the fire. They smelled a lot better anyway. Thank goodness it was a hot day. They would finish drying while I wore them.

I drove the car to Doncaster's main shopping area. I parked in Frenchgate Street and trudged damply and unwillingly into the Marks and Spencer store. It was as I was walking through the revolving doors that I came reluctantly to a decision. I decided to do as Elise suggested, and get some assistance. It went severely against the grain to ask for help, but it was the lesser of two evils. I summoned up my courage, and I flagged down a passing shop assistant. She was a motherly kind of person with a comfortable, rounded sort of figure and a kind face. The sort a chap in trouble might trust. I showed her the paper.

'It's stuff for my er, my sister. She n-needs some new clothes, but she's er, got flu. S-so, she sent m-me,' I lied. I must have been as red as a beetroot because I could feel my face burning. I prayed she wouldn't notice my embarrassment…She noticed.

'OK, love,' she said in that broad South Yorkshire accent. 'Leave it to me. Have you got more things to buy?' I nodded. 'I'll leave these at the checkout for you. What's your name?'

'Er, Ph-Eddie.' For I had remembered just in time that my signature was E. White!'

'OK, Eddie. I'll make sure your *sister* is happy with her new clothes. The assistant at the till will put them by in your name.' I'm sure she had more than a suspicion that Elise was no relation of mine whatsoever. She went off with the list, trying hard not to smile.

I got some stuff of my own. I upgraded my underwear. There was at that time a temporary, and frankly awful, fashion for brushed nylon pants. Yes, really! Nylon for God's sake, around your unmentionable parts! My mother thought she was helping me to be fashionable. She bought some for me, along with my usual boring plain white briefs. The nylon was certainly colourful. I remember a bright purple pair, but it was awful to wear. It itched and made you sweat.

I selected for myself some nice new, comfortable briefs, in various colours, and, remembering what Elise had said, definitely not boring old white. And cotton, not nylon! I also bought some new trousers, a polo-neck shirt and some t-shirts, and two pairs of smart but casual sneakers.

When I'd finished, I went to the till. My heart sank. Behind the counter the assistant was much nearer my own age – a teenager. Shyly, I asked her for the things put aside for Eddie.

'Oh. Here you are, *Eddie*,' she mocked. She couldn't keep the smirk off her face nor out of her voice. The other lady must have told her of my embarrassment in graphic detail. She got Elise's clothes out of a carrier bag and put them with mine on the counter. I looked away, trying to look casual. She rang every item up at the till. There were no barcodes in those days. She had to look at the price label and push the appropriate buttons for the price. With every click-click whirr-click, I became more embarrassed. Finally, the torture came to an end.

'With your clothes as well, that's eighteen pounds, eleven shillings and sixpence altogether, sir.'

Eighteen pounds! That was more than my dad's weekly wage. I gulped a bit, then handed over the American Express card.

Her attitude changed instantly. She became a bit more respectful.

'Thank you, sir. Just a moment.' She put the card,

with a slip of paper in a machine, swiped a handle backward and forward, and put the slip on the counter for me to sign. I wrote the signature I had practised back at the house. I tried to write it as casually as I could manage. I stood sweating while she looked at the payment slip.

After what seemed like a couple of hours, but was probably only a few seconds, she tore off the top copy, handed me the slip and smiled. 'Bye then, *Mr Eddie*,' she said. I left, with my two carrier bags.

I exited the store at high speed, carrying my purchases. Apart from that brief glimpse, I hadn't even looked at the clothes the woman had selected for Elise, I just prayed that they were OK. Once outside I leaned back against the wall and breathed heavily for a few moments. What an ordeal.

When I got back, Elise was sitting at the dining room table. It was littered with sheets and scraps of paper. She had been translating all sorts of documents into English.

'Me-byet,' she said, or that's what it sounded like to me. 'That's "hello" in Russian. Look, I think I've found something.' She waved one of the pieces of paper scattered around her on the table. 'When we were training, we were told that the Russian bureaucracy is ten times worse than even our own bureaucracy. They have to write down everything in triplicate, then record in triplicate everything they've actually written down. 'They can't take a... they can't go to the toilet without permission. Look at this.'

She showed me the paper. It had Russian writing on it, with her translation underneath. 'At the top, that's an English address, with *безопасныйдом*' (it sounded like 'visa-parsley dome') 'the Russian words for "safe house". This is a list of groceries bought there. They have to have their expenses approved, same as we do.'

'OK,' I replied, trying to look intelligent. I must confess I was so totally pre-occupied with worrying about the purchases, that I couldn't concentrate on minor matters like what the Russians were up to. *They* hadn't asked me to buy clothes!

'Now look at these dates. They suddenly start buying more food for the safe house on the twenty-fifth of July.'

'Wasn't that…'

'The night we met? Yes, it was.' She turned back to the paperwork. 'More than twice as much food. Do you see what this means?'

'Erm. Oh.' Now I really did feel like Watson under the stern gaze of Holmes! I forced myself to address the question, wrenching my thoughts away from the shopping. 'Er, well, perhaps they were expecting more agents, or, erm…'

'Yes. Go on, or what?'

Light dawned at last.' Oh, I see what you mean. They were expecting "guests". Your lot!'

'Yes, "my lot". The trainees. That means they were

alive. Well, then. You don't need extra food for corpses. If they're still alive, it's ten to one they are in this house.'

Her eyes shone at the thought that her colleagues might still be alive.

'Maybe we should phone the Whirlwind lady and tell her, I'm sure she'd like to know.'

'I tried while you were out. The number is no longer in service.' She pulled a face. 'I expected it, actually. If the service has been penetrated no one is safe. Everyone must be considered suspect, including us. She is covering her own back. She will ring the safe houses in turn, but we can't wait. We have to go now – today.' She looked up at me. 'How do you feel about this, Phil? About being on our own? It could be really dangerous. I know about Mr Gray now, but at the same time the opposition will know I'm on the loose. If they think I know about their safe house, they will move; they might even kill the trainees and,' she gulped, 'Sigma One. We need to get to this *безопасныйдом*, this Russian safe house, ASAP.' She indicated the paper she was translating 'like, yesterday…Look, Phil…I can go on my own?'

'No!' I gasped. I was horrified. 'I want to come with you. You can't leave me behind now!' I might have raised my voice a bit in my vehemence.

She gave that smile again. A warm, fuzzy feeling spread right through me. She came over to me, squeezed my hand and kissed me lightly on the lips. She created havoc in my heart and body then, disappointingly, she pulled away – all business.

'Right, give me my clothes. What did you get me? Let me see.'

This was the moment I had been dreading. No putting it off any longer. I closed my eyes crossed my fingers very tightly, and said a silent prayer, as she burrowed into the Marks and Sparks bag.

'Wow!' That was promising. I opened an eye. She turned and looked at me. 'These are nice things. You must have spent some money.' She was holding up bra and pants. I closed my eyes. She giggled.

'It came to eighteen pounds or so, with my stuff.'

She shrugged off the expense. 'It's really nice. My colours too, how did you know?' She kissed me again, on the cheek this time.

'Well, I'd better get into this stuff. I'll be back in one minute.' She took the clothes and left for her bedroom.

Actually, it was more like three minutes but still remarkably quick. Quicker than me. I got out of my damp clothes and into my new ones right there in the living room, in front of the nice warm fire. I dressed in frantic haste; in case she should come back before I was ready. I used the dressing gown as a sort of beach robe... I was still pulling on my nice new t-shirt as she came in silently, as usual. She moved as quietly as a cat. I didn't see her arrive, being tangled up in the shirt. I didn't know she was there.

When I emerged through the top of the t-shirt, I was startled to find her looking at me, appraisingly.

'You have a nice body,' she observed. I grappled my way into the shirt, crimson with embarrassment for the umpteenth time that day.

'It's t-too s-skinny,' I replied. 'The other kids call me t-tin-ribs!'

'It's fine. Like Mick Jagger. Those clothes look good on you. Yes, a great improvement.' She came over and helped me to pull my shirt down. 'Nice shirt, too.'

'Th-thanks,' was all I could say at first. Then I managed, 'Y-You look good too.'

She did; good enough to eat, in fact. Her clear complexion was rosy pink with the excitement of the task in hand and with hurrying into her clothes. Now that her red hair was clean, and dry, it shone. She had put it up into a ponytail. Her new clothes fitted perfectly. She wore a polo neck with broad navy-blue stripes, and blue slacks. She laughed. She did a twirl so I could see the full, enchanting picture. Then, putting the rest of our nice new clothes in the back of the car, we were off.

— CHAPTER NINETEEN —
Agent on Fire

'Where are we going?' I asked as we jumped into the car. My speed was improving. I was actually in my seat with the door closed before the Mini shot away from the kerb. It was almost twelve o'clock.

'London.'

'A1 all the way,' I said.

'The address is in Hornsey, that's in north London.'

'That's good.'

'Is it? Why?'

'We'll get there a bit quicker than if it was south London,' I pointed out, quite reasonably, I thought. She rolled her eyes.

Once more we were on the road. This time we were better dressed for the part. Outside Sandy, we stopped for lunch at a Happy Eater; it was nearly two by now. I caught a glimpse of the two of us, reflected in the windows of the restaurant, as we approached the entrance. We looked, I thought, like an illustration from a fashion magazine. A before and after advert. I was the 'before' and she was the 'after'. She wore her clothes well, I…not so well.

After eating, we pressed on. I felt fab. I was in the throes of love, and I was riding high. The only fly in the ointment, was that we didn't know what we were going to find when we got to the safe house. I was driving as we entered the outskirts of London.

'OK, the address we want is not too far from the A1,' Elise navigated. 'We need to turn left onto Hornsey Lane, just before Archway.'

So, I did. We steered our way to a suburban street in Hornsey, called Rokesly Avenue.

'Hey, that rhymes with Dokesley!' she exclaimed. 'I'm guessing that means "rook's meadow", what d'you think?'

I smiled nervously at her. 'I think you're right,' I croaked, sounding remarkably rook-like.

'Nervous?'

I nodded.

'Me too,' she agreed. All I could think was that, if she was nervous, she was hiding it remarkably well. If anything, she looked excited. Her eyes were shining, her cheeks were pink. At that moment she looked like the most beautiful girl I had ever seen. Sarah Miles, pah! Sarah who?

We parked the car at the top of the avenue, and we made our way on foot, arm in arm, to number thirty-four. It was a large house on a corner. We went up the street, alongside the house, to get a good idea of the lie of the land. Behind the house, the ground sloped steeply upwards. There must have been at least three floors above ground, and a basement as well with windows at the front, below the level of the garden. The garden was very small at the front, but huge at the back, and it was in a total mess. There were trees, and there was a lawn, badly scuffed and bare in patches. There were pieces of wood from packing cases, cardboard from boxes, paper and bits of rope and string all over the place. From the labels on the packaging material, it seemed to be from furniture they had bought for the house. When they unpacked everything, they must have thrown all the packaging into the garden pell-mell. Lazy beggars.

'If they're still alive, they're in that house somewhere,' Elise commented.

We didn't linger. We walked back down to the avenue, and on past. Her words, so casually spoken, made me think. They rang in my ears, *If they're still alive...* I prayed that they were.

We stopped and looked back at the house from further down the road.

'There will be at least three of the opposition, maybe more,' she said, thoughtfully. I nodded and swallowed hard. What could we two do against three, four or more pistol-packing Russian agents?

'Let's go and have a coffee and think, now that we've seen the house,' I suggested. Anything to put off the evil hour. Elise was all on fire to charge in and beat up some people, but I was terrified that it might be us that got beaten, or even shot, unless we could come up with a plan. We went to a café near the Crouch End clocktower.

'Show me the paper where they order groceries again,' I said, after we had sat down and ordered coffee. I hadn't an idea in my head, but Elise was gazing at me with that trusting look, and those huge green eyes. I had to do something! I looked at the paper for a moment without really seeing it, then things began to come into focus. I concentrated, and I looked more closely. I read her translation, hastily scribbled alongside the Russian.

'Look at the bread,' I chimed. 'They paid for three loaves on the twenty-first of July, then on the twenty-fifth, they paid for six loaves.'

'All right. I see that, but I don't see how that helps us?'

'Well, there are four prisoners, right? Sigma One, Mr Black, Mr Green, and Mr Brown. We know Mr Gray was in Scotland, waiting for someone to contact him, so he's not included in this.'

'Waiting for *me* to contact him. They must have realised I'd slipped the net, and they left him there to wait for my call. What a fool I was to ring him and give our position away,' she remarked, bitterly.

'You weren't to know,' I said, rather generously, I thought. 'But look, d'you see? *Twice* as much bread. Four more people, it means that there are no more than three or four people looking after them.'

'Yes. Yes, I think you're right. I also think we can assume that they wouldn't be so lavish with the prisoners' rations, so it's back to the usual triad. Three agents. Three of them, and four prisoners. And us. Six of us and three of them. Two to one. Pretty good odds. OK, but how do we get into the house? D'you think there's a fire alarm in there? We could set it off.'

'You're obsessed with fire alarms,' I said, witheringly. But her obsession sparked an idea in my brain. 'Maybe we *can* create an alarming fire though,' I murmured thoughtfully, remembering all the rubbish in the garden. I could see how my fire-making abilities could be of use once more.

'We need a can of petrol, some matches, and, and night-time.'

'Attaboy, Phil-Will! Now you're speaking my language. Let's give it to them! When they come out, we'll shoot them one by one...' She looked at my horrified face. 'I mean, we'll grab them one by one and tie them up!'

'Right!' I doubted.

By now it was after four o'clock in the afternoon. It wouldn't be dark for more than five hours.

'Well,' she said with that cheeky raised eyebrow, 'Miss Moneypenny, what are we going to do for five hours?'

I shrugged. She sighed and rolled her eyes. 'Oh well... I bet James Bond never had this problem!'

I had no idea what she meant. She smiled at me. She came over to my seat and ruffled my hair. 'There must be a library,' she said. 'Why don't we both find a good book. You could read some James Bond.'

There was indeed a library, in a magnificent old building. It was called Hornsey Library. I found the James Bond books. I was happily occupied for quite some time. She read one, too. She kept sniggering, which was annoying.

At seven o'clock the library closed, and we were turfed out. We went for a walk in Priory Park, at the bottom of Rokesly avenue. We found a park bench where we rested in the warm evening sunshine and talked, or sat in companionable silence, until the park closed at nine.

She was remarkably easy to talk to. I told her about my life so far, my clumsiness, my lack of friends, lack of girlfriends, my shyness. She was very understanding. She knew all about feeling different. She told me about her life. Her parents were divorced. Her father had run off with a younger woman. Her mother had taken to drink. Elise had taken on the role of man of the household from an early age; and she had been forced to act as mother to her own mother. No wonder she was such a tough character. She'd had to be strong. She was a fusion of male and female toughness. She, too, found it hard to fit in, either with female, or male, friends. 'I'm neither fish nor fowl…' she said.

'Nor good red herring,' I finished the saying.

'What?'

'Never mind,' I said, and I changed the subject. 'Your grandmother sounds like an amazing person. I think she would be proud of you.' She blushed. I could tell she was pleased.

All too soon, it was time to go to work. As they were closing the park gates, we transferred to a pub. I sat in there with my customary half of lager and lime, definitely no wine. My head still ached thinking about the last time!

Elise went to a petrol station and bought a gallon of petrol in a can, some matches, and several bags of coke – not the drink, the coal; it burns without smoke. It's mainly used for barbecues these days, but in those days, it was burned for fuel. Leaving the flammables in the car, she joined me in the pub.

'OK, this is your show, plan-man, now what?'

'We wait until it's completely dark, preferably until they've gone to bed.'

'They'll leave at least one of them on watch, all night.'

'That's OK, it shouldn't make any difference,' I said, crossing my fingers behind my back. 'They will all come out if there's a fire.'

'Erm, I don't want to interfere,' she said, hesitantly. 'But how do we stop the fire getting out of control? We don't want to immolate our friends along with our enemies!'

I shared my idea. 'The fire will be in the back

garden. Not too close to the house. If we make it big enough, they will come out to see what's happening. Then you can round them up with your gun.'

'Suppose they just look out of the window and decide it's safe enough to leave it?'

'I'm going to make sure that they can't ignore it! Anyway, there is a plan B.'

She gave me an inquisitive look. 'Plan B?'

There wasn't a plan B. Now I had to think of something, quickly. Sitting there, with my lager and lime, I had to think on my seat.

'Er, I knock on the door and when they answer I tell them there is a bad fire in the back garden…And I've phoned the fire brigade. That should worry them, they won't want to explain things to the authorities, I bet! You stand by to do your thing. You can let your inner tigress off her leash.' I grinned.

She smiled back. 'Rawr!'

Darkness fell at about half past nine. We waited in the pub until closing time at eleven, then we made our way back to Rokesly avenue. It had been a long day, but I felt wide awake. I was buoyed up by the excitement of the quest ahead of us.

Because the house was on a corner, it made access to the garden that little bit easier. Elise parked the car in the steeply sloped side street, alongside number thirty-four. I helped her to carry the petrol and the bags of coke from the car and we took them into the garden. We pushed through a gap in the hedge, dropped the flammables and then looked around. The garden was so dimly lit; it would be near impossible for anyone in the house to see us. As my eyes adjusted, I looked around. I noted afresh just how much rubbish there was for burning. It made my job so much easier.

I looked for a good spot. The fire would have to be close enough to the house to cause a fright, but not close enough to be dangerous. Then I picked my spot and got to work. Under the cover of darkness, using stealth – and the materials scattered all over the garden – I was able to build a very respectable bonfire. No alarm came from the house. So far, we had managed the whole thing without being spotted.

'Some lookout they're keeping,' muttered Elise. She was leaning against a tree. Almost invisible in the deep purple shade of its summer leaves and branches, she stood on guard duty and watched me work.

I assembled the bonfire in layers. Paper and card went at the bottom to act as kindling, with a little bit of petrol. The coke came next, with a little more petrol over it to get it started, then all the wood I could find. Finally, more card and paper, which I had to put on top of the fire on tiptoe; it was so high. I sloshed the remaining petrol – the best part of a gallon– over the top of the heap, where it lay in puddles on the paper and card, dripping down onto the heaped material beneath. I applied a match to the base. The results exceeded my wildest expectations.

As the petrol-damped paper at the bottom caught,

the fire took hold with a WHOOMPH! It almost singed my eyebrows. I recoiled away from the flames and fell down backwards. Out of the corner of my eye I saw Elise with her mouth open. She shook herself out of her trance, came over and dragged me away from the blaze. She was shaking her head in disbelief, her eyes wide at the spectacle unfolding in the garden.

'You know, it's a pleasure to watch your work,' she acknowledged, finally.

In literally a few seconds the fire was burning high and fierce. It was so fierce that I thought it couldn't possibly get brighter or hotter. Then something happened that changed the whole scenario, turning the garden into a species of hell.

With the height and the sudden ferocity of the fire, it was not surprising that it was only burning for about a minute, before someone in the house noticed. There was a shout. There was a moment's pause. In that pause, Elise moved like lightning. In less than two seconds she was poised, gun in hand, crouching by the steps leading down from the back door. Her grim expression was illuminated by the red light of the massive conflagration we'd started. I squatted down behind a tree, and peeped round to watch. By now the fire was assaulting all our senses, with its heat on our skin, its fiery brightness in our eyes, the crackling noise of the blazing wood in our ears, and the tang of petrol-assisted burning up our noses and in our mouths.

A man rushed out of the house with a bucket of water and ran down the steps. He was in his trousers, braces and shirtsleeves, and bare-footed. He heaved the bucket of water over the fire. Water on a petrol fire. It was the worst thing he could have done. The only result was to splash the burning petrol all over the garden. Trees caught fire, the sparse grass began to burn, and the bonfire surged brighter and hotter, like a wild fiery beast–a dragon, awoken from its sleep, and now very angry.

He stood, shocked, trying to work out what he had done. The fire was getting completely out of hand. He had got splashed with some of the petrol, and his arms were smouldering. Frantically he smacked at them to put himself out. He staggered back from the inferno, bucket still in his hand. Of the three of us out there, Elise was the first to recover. She silently crept up behind the man, who was still frantically patting his arms.

'*положитьруки вверх,*' she snapped. Taken completely by surprise – one more shock in what was turning out to be a very bad night – he spun round, started in amazement, goggled at her for a moment as if she was some sort of alien thing, then finally he obeyed. He raised his smoking arms towards the sky. His attention was still focused on the flames; by now the whole garden seemed to be ablaze. His face was aghast and ghostly in the lurid light, mouth gaping open, completely transfixed by this glimpse of Hell.

'*позвонитьим, чтобывыйти,*' ordered Elise.

The man was in no state to refuse. Badly shaken by events, he obediently turned and called out to his colleagues for help. When he had done that, Elise, moved behind him and scientifically clobbered him on the back of his head with the pistol. He went down like the proverbial pole-axed bullock.

'You haven't killed him, have you?' I hissed, from my refuge, in the shadows behind the burning tree.

She wrung her hand 'Ow,' she hissed. 'With that skull? He'll be asleep for a while, that's all. Quick, when they come out, stick your leg out, we'll trip them down the steps.'

In the end we found a better way. Some of the packing material had escaped being put on the fire; there were several pieces of rope. I held one up. She nodded her approval. We quickly got into position on either side of the steps up to the back door. We held one end of the rope each. Two more men came out to the top of the steps and gazed in amazement. These two were in their pyjamas. They stood and stared, open-mouthed, at the violent conflagration in the garden. One of them shouted and pointed to their colleague, unconscious at the bottom of the steps, they hurried towards him. We pulled the rope hard, so that it was taut and just below knee height. They were in such a rush they didn't notice it. They didn't stand a chance. The rope tripped them, and they crashed heavily down the steps. Before they could even begin to recover themselves, Elise dealt with them – methodically and efficiently– before using the rope to tie them up.

'It's a pleasure to watch your work,' I said, imitating her accent.

'Was that supposed to be me?' She laughed. Then she hugged me for sheer relief and pleasure in a job well done. 'Good teamwork,' she murmured in my ear. 'You wait here. I'm going to search the house.'

— CHAPTER TWENTY —
Agents Rescued

Elise slipped inside the back door, warily, gun in hand. With nothing to do but wait, I thought it might be a good idea to collect the guns from the men in the garden. I cautiously tiptoed around them as if they were sleeping lions. I needn't have worried; Elise had done her job well. None of them so much as stirred. I relieved them of their weapons, then I sat on one of the steps and waited – watching the garden burning away. It was almost a pity I didn't smoke; I could really have used one of Bond's Moreland cigarettes.

I waited for a couple of minutes longer, but when nothing happened, I began to get restless. The three men were out for the count and trussed up like oven-ready turkeys. It was all quiet in the house, and out here – apart from the fire, still crackling away. It was burning less fiercely by now, and it was rapidly becoming less interesting to watch. After waiting another couple of minutes, I decided to follow Elise into the house, to see what was happening. I couldn't bear to be away from her, if the truth be told. Besides, I felt I was missing the action. I wanted to be there when the team was rescued.

I sauntered in, got halfway through the kitchen, then froze. I could hear a male voice speaking, and it didn't sound friendly. I crept past the stone sink and the Belling cooker and peeped round the door. There was Elise, standing in the hallway, with her hands in the air. Behind her, with his back to me, was a youngish man with his gun in one hand and hers in the other. I ducked back, my heart pounding.

'Well, well, well. Lambda Three. Haven't you done well, *Elise*,' he mock congratulated. 'But what did they tell us, never, ever drop your guard! You always were the impetuous member of the group. Now you're in the soup. Finally, we have the whole lot of you in the bag.'

Elise was remarkably calm. 'That's a mixed metaphor. "In the pan" would have been better than "in the bag".'

He became nastier. 'Either way, you're in it. Now move!'

'Where?'

'You're going to join your friends.' She didn't move.

'One question, Jack. Why? Why betray your country, your friends?'

The scales fell from my eyes. This was Jack, the trainee codenamed Mr Gray. He was the extra man, not accounted for in the list of supplies; probably because he had only recently arrived from Scotland.

'Money, of course,' he replied. 'And lots of it. Now move!'

Quick, quick, what to do, what to do? I asked myself; I was in a complete tizzy. Various options flitted through my mind. *Run away,* said a little voice inside me. It was drowned out. *Time to step up to the mark, Q! 007 is down. Up to you now,* my better-self said. I was calling my own bluff.

I removed one of the guns from my pocket, as quietly as I could. I took several deep breaths, in an effort to build up my courage. It wasn't working. I was, and remained, petrified. But Elise was in trouble. Channelling James Bond as well as I was able, heart pounding like a steam hammer, I leaped out into the hall, pointed the gun at the man and screamed, 'PUT YOUR HANDS UP!' at the top of my voice. Because I was so nervous, it came out a lot louder than I had intended. The decibel level must have been off the scale! A sergeant-major on the parade ground, on hearing it, would have taken off his hat to me; and then resigned and hung up his shiny boots.

Mr Gray was taken completely by surprise. He shied like a startled horse. He turned; hand clasped to his chest in shock. He saw me, in full crouching James Bond stance, pointing the gun at him. He hesitated, breathing heavily, before putting up his hands.

Elise smiled, and addressed him: 'What did they

tell us in training? Never underestimate your enemy.' She looked at me, and with an impish smile. 'Well done, er, Mr Lavender!' Her expression changed again; now it was somewhere between grim and murderous. A bit like Ernst Stavro Blofeld when a henchman told him Bond had escaped…again.

Mr Gray eyed me and shrugged. He offered his gun to Elise. 'They're not paying me enough to be a hero,' he stated. Elise took the gun, and kept it trained on him. She edged over, never taking her eyes off the traitor, and took my gun. I was only too glad to hand it over, but then she gave me *her* gun.

She ordered him to sit down. 'Cover him, Mr Lavender,' she told me. 'If he even breathes too enthusiastically, shoot him!' her anger was cold and terrifying. It frightened me, let alone Jack. This youth had betrayed her and all the other trainees – just for money. While I covered him, somewhat nervously, she slipped the surplus gun in her jacket pocket, and proceeded to tie his hands. She gagged him, and, as an afterthought, she blindfolded him.

I helped her with him as she made him walk up the stairs to one of the bedrooms. It was not an easy job, as he couldn't see. She wasn't gentle. She didn't care how many times he stumbled against the banisters or banged his head against the wall. Once in the disordered bedroom, she pushed him down onto the bed, tied his legs, and left him lying there. We came out and she shut the door.

She leaned against the door, closed her eyes and breathed heavily for a few moments. Then she turned to me and threw her arms around me. After a moment she broke away. 'Oh, you darling!' she exclaimed. 'He really had the drop on me. How did you know to come in?' She didn't wait for an answer. 'Never mind, I'm just glad you did. You know the only thing that would have made it better?'

I shook my head, as she smiled at me. To my surprise, she was smiling through tears. She showed me the gun I had used to hold Jack up. 'The only thing to make it better would have been if you had taken the safety catch off!'

She hugged me again and laughed, then burst into tears. It made me realise just what a strain she had been under. Tough as old boots on the outside but, at times, vulnerable as a kitten on the inside. Tears pricked my eyes as well, as I hugged her back, wholeheartedly. After a moment or two, she broke away, shook her head and comically banged her ears.

She swore, 'what a foghorn of a voice you have! I think you've deafened me,' she joked, and smiled broadly. 'I'm not complaining though, did you see him jump? Come on, let's find the others. I hope to god they're still alive.' She indicated the bedroom door behind which Mr Gray was stewing. 'He'd better hope so too!' She positively snarled the last remark.

We started down the stairs. 'Just one thing,' I said. '*Mr Lavender*, really?'

'Well, I was looking at you and it was the only colour I could think of.'

'Thanks, that makes it worse!'

'Cheer up; it could have been worse still, it could have been puce! Mr Puce, what d'you think?'

'I think I prefer Mr Lavender.'

We began a methodical search of the house. Elise was beginning to grow into the part of Sigma One; she seemed completely at ease in the role. We started our search at the top of the house, and I went with her all the way. I had no intention of letting her out of my sight again.

The other bedrooms were a complete mess, where the Russians had leapt out of their beds to go and help their comrade, but there was no one there. The ground floor was empty too.

'The basement, ' Elise suggested.

There was a door in the hall. We went through it and found some steps into the basement. Elise had learned a little caution by now, and went slowly, with her gun held out in front of her. The steps were lit by a single electric light. I found the switch and turned it on. Down the stairs was a very short corridor at the end of which was a closed door.

Elise went cautiously down a few steps, her gun at the ready. 'Hello?' she called. Is anybody there? Kappa Three, Omega Three, are you there?'

There was a sort of inarticulate, faint cry from somewhere at the bottom of the stairs. She took the rest of the stairs in a flying leap and ran to the door. I winced as she landed with a crash, absorbing the impact with bent knees. I walked carefully down after her, very carefully… well, those stairs were steep!

Elise tried the door. It was locked. I came up to her. 'The saint would shoot the lock off,' I said.

'Yes, and probably end up shooting the people in there!' she replied.

'I'll charge it down.' I boasted. After all, how hard could it be? The Saint did it all the time on the telly! She watched with a sceptical look on her face as I prepared myself, then shoulder-charged the door.

Oh my god, it hurt; I mean it *really* hurt. I thought my shoulder was broken! I was convinced it would never be the same again. I felt dizzy with the pain and my legs went wobbly. The door, on the other hand wasn't damaged at all; I could positively feel it sneering at me.

Elise sighed, rolled her eyes and shook her head. 'Wait there.' She disappeared up the stairs back into the main part of the house. She was gone quite some time. I moaned quietly and tried to massage my shoulder, which protested in no uncertain terms. Finally, Elise came back with a small bunch of keys that she had found in the kitchen. The door opened at the second try. I leaned against the door lintel and massaged my poor arm and shoulder. She gave me a wry smile.

'Poor you,' she soothed. I shrugged, and then

groaned. Shrugging was going to be painful for some time!

The room we entered was a lounge, with a sofa and easy chairs. It had a large window, through which we could see the garden wall. Then, some five feet up, was the garden. Through net curtains, the dying embers of the fire were still visible, glowing red and orange. Inside the room, there were four men tied up and lying on thin mattresses. The three younger ones, teenagers by the look of them, didn't look in bad shape, but the older guy, a man of about thirty, had obviously been badly beaten.

Elise flew to his side. 'Mr Plum!' she exclaimed. He looked bruised and bloody; he seemed unable to respond to her. The others brightened up and reacted when they saw us, but the former Sigma One lay apathetically on his mattress. All the prisoners were bound and gagged. Elise went down on her knees to care for Mr Plum. I was studying the *Merchant of Venice* at school. I now understood, at painful first-hand, the full meaning of Shakespeare's phrase '*As doubtful thoughts, and rash-embraced despair, and shuddering fear, and green-eyed jealousy!*' as I watched Elise tenderly ministering to Mr Plum, with tears running freely down her cheeks.

With a desperate ache in my heart, I set about freeing her other friends. I first removed their gags.

'They didn't get you then,' acknowledged one of the trainees to Elise. A black kid

Tears were flowing freely down Elise's face. 'No.' She shook her head and smiled though her tears. 'They didn't get me! I got them!'

'Sigma One was strong,' continued the black kid – Mr Green, I learned later. 'They took him out and worked on him, but he wouldn't tell them anything. They gave up on him and they had just started on us, but we don't know anything, how could we?' He burst into tears, and Elise came over, put her arms round him and consoled him. The whole team looked very young. They had obviously been chosen because of their youthful looks; none was older than seventeen.

Soon the prisoners were all free. We all climbed out of the cellar, Elise going first, with her gun in hand, ready for anything. She looked terrifying – and magnificent. My heart lurched again.

Together with Mr Green, whose real name was Daniel, I helped the former Sigma One up the steps. We pretty much carried him. It was hard going. We managed to get out onto the street without further incident, and the other two limped after us. Once out on the pavement, we could hear a siren going. It seemed someone had phoned the authorities after all. The fire brigade was on its way. I wasn't surprised. That bonfire would have awakened the dead.

'Seems like plan B is happening after all,' said Elise, smiling grimly. 'Do you want to knock on the door and tell them, or shall I?' I could only smile and shake my head. We put on some haste. We got Mr Plum into the car, in the front passenger seat.

'You drive, Mr. Lavender,' Elise declared. My chest swelled… my head swelled as well!

Before she got into the back seat, Elise spoke to the other three.

'Make your way to this safe house,' she told them and gave them the address of one of the four houses, the one nearest to London, which was in Hertford. 'Here's some money.' She gave them two ten pound notes! That would keep my family going for more than a month.

'This should be enough to get you there by train. There's a railway station I noticed down the road. Wait at the house for me to contact you. Stay low. The password is "Whirlwind". Don't speak to anyone who doesn't use this password. I've been given the designation Sigma One. Look after each other's wounds as best you can. There are first aid boxes in all of the safe houses.'

'What are you going to do, Sigma One?' asked Mr Green. It was the first time anyone had addressed Elise by her new rank.

'Mr Lavender and I are going to take Sig…that is, Mr Plum, to hospital. Now go, quickly, before the authorities get here!'

We left them on the pavement. They set off, as fast as they could go in their bruised and battered condition, for Hornsey station. This, I learned later, would take them to Moorgate, from where they all got a train to Hertford North station, and the safe house.

Elise watched them go. A few minutes later, we set off for the Whittington Hospital, just down the road from where we were. It was marked on the A to Z. As we turned out of Rokesly Avenue, the fire engine was just turning in.

I couldn't help feeling resentful as Elise continued to fuss tenderly over the former Sigma One. Mr Plum was put in the front seat of the Mini. It didn't look as though she had got over her 'teenage crush' to my jealous eyes. We delivered him to A and E, and waited until he was taken in to be examined. We were forced to lie to the hospital staff. We told the nurse who admitted him, that we didn't know who he was, and that we had found him on the street in Tottenham in this beaten up condition.

'Maybe he was mugged?' Elise speculated to the nurse. Confident that he was being looked after, we slipped away before the police could get involved.

As I drove, Elise discussed her plans.

'I gave them all the phone number, but not the address, of the safe house in Doncaster. We'll go back there now.' She hesitated. 'That means I can drop you off back at home, um, if you'd like?'

She saw my face. 'Well, Phil-Will,' she said, more urgently, 'you have to go home some time, or your parents will wonder what on earth has happened to you.' She paused. 'And I have to go back to the safe house. The boss lady will be contacting each of the safe houses in turn, and I have to be there.'

'P-Please, Elise, d-don't send me away.' My stutter was back! I was devastated at the thought of the adventure being over; that my time with her might be coming to an end. I was also upset at the thought that the sight of Mr Plum, hurt and in need of her, might have re-ignited her feelings for him.

She hesitated, and I pressed home my attack. 'Anyway, it's t-too soon to go back. Remember, my cover story is that I'm camping in the Lake District for a few days. It's only been three so far. Besides, the lady might want to talk to the civilian who was with you.' I could see that shot, at least, had hit the target. She gave in gracefully.

'OK,' she agreed and smiled. 'I'm glad.' She put her hand on mine and squeezed it gently. 'Thank you,' she said. I was mystified.

'What for?'

'For being you.' Now I *was* confused! Just to add to all my other feelings of love, jealousy, desperation and heartache.

'Come on,' she went on, 'let's head back to Doncaster. We can sleep and have a bit of a rest. What an evening! You could say that this part of the mission has gone with a bang. I can't believe what you did with that fire. Did you know it would do that?'

I had to be honest. 'No, I was as shocked as anybody.'

'No, you weren't! Not as shocked as that Russian.'

She giggled. 'He just stood there, with the bucket dangling in his hand, like he had seen a ghost, or a hundred ghosts.'

We both went quiet for a bit. I negotiated the streets of North London and we headed out of the city towards Doncaster and home.

— CHAPTER TWENTY-ONE —
Agent Says Goodbye

The journey north was completed largely in thoughtful silence. We were both exhausted. It was five o'clock in the morning. By the time we got back to Doncaster, we had been awake for almost twenty-four hours. The sun's light was visible as it started to come up from below the horizon. In the broadening dawn light, we trudged back into the house, completely spent. I was glad Elise had let me come back with her. Apart from all the other considerations, I still had to replace the tent and sleeping bags.

We slept for around six hours and woke at about midday. Rather than eat the sparse rations provided in the safe house, we went into the centre of Doncaster for a meal out. We ate at the restaurant in British Home Stores (later to become BHS.) Then we went to Millets, where Elise insisted on buying me some new camping equipment – top of the range.

'You keep buying me things. I can't give you anything,' I protested as Elise paid yet again.

'I'm not paying, the service is.' She winked and then planted a kiss on my cheek. 'And anyway, you deserve it.'

We went back to the house for the afternoon.

Elise was very pensive. She seemed uncomfortable. Eventually she spoke. 'Erm, Phil. Look, um…' I held my breath and waited; a cold thrill went through my body; my heart began to beat faster. I dreaded what she was about to say.

'Look. Don't get me wrong. This has been great, but you are going to have to go home at some point. When the boss lady has phoned, we'll have to make up our minds what we are going to do.'

'It sounds like you have made up your mind,' I pouted.

She came and sat next to me on the sofa. She intertwined her fingers in mine and leaned her head on my shoulder. After sitting stiffly for a moment, I relented, and I put my arm around her.

'Please, Phil. Don't make this any harder than it has to be…I mean, I like you…a lot. But right now, well, I can't afford to have any distractions if I'm to become an agent.'

'Elise…I th-think I love you.'

She looked up at me. Tears started in her eyes. She swallowed. 'You know, I really thought I would feel wonderful the first time someone said that to me, like walking on air, but I feel miserable. Right now, my emotions are so mixed up I don't know what I'm feeling.'

'It's Mr Plum, isn't it? Seeing him again, like that...'

'No! Yes. Maybe. Oh, I don't know.' A tear rolled down her cheek. 'I do really like you, Phil—'

'So, what's the problem?'

'It's not just Mr Plum, seeing him all hurt and vulnerable like that. I do still have confused feelings about him. But it's not just that. It's everything. It's life. Life is the problem. You have your life and I have mine, and they're miles apart, in more than just geography.'

Tears were running down my face now. 'P-please, don't say th-that it's over.' Damn that stammer of mine!

She put her arms around me, pulled my head onto her shoulder and rocked me as if I were a baby. 'Oh, Phil-Will. Look, maybe in a little while, we can meet up again. If we still feel the same way, then...well let's take it from there.'

'P-Promise?' My voice came out as a squeak.

She smiled at me through her tears. 'Cross my heart and hope to die.'

She kissed me on the lips, and I kissed her back with more enthusiasm than skill.

She gently pulled away, 'Ouch! I can see I'm going to have bruised lips if I'm going to be snogging you.' She smiled brightly.

'Sorry. That was my first real kiss.'

'I would never have guessed.' We both laughed. We each wiped away our tears. The mardy clouds over my head cleared a little, and a more cheerful sun began to peep through. I felt a little better. She put her hand up and stroked my face. She smiled and came closer. We looked into each other's eyes. My heart beat faster and my breathing became ragged. At that moment the phone rang. Damn the thing! She sprang up to answer it. The magical moment was gone.

'Hello, do you have a weather report for me?' she asked briskly. She was every inch Sigma One now. I came up to her and she held the phone so we could both hear it.

'Whirlwind.'

'This is Sigma One reporting, I'm going to scrambler.' She pressed a button on the device next to the phone, totally the competent professional. She continued, 'Mr Green, Mr Brown, and Mr Blue are now safe. I was able to extract them from the Russian safe house. They were being held and tortured for information. They are in the safe house in Hertford. As far as I know, no one told the enemy anything, but I can't be sure. Mr. Plum was badly hurt and is in hospital, but I think he'll recover.'

There was silence at the other end for a short while. 'How was this achieved?'

Elise smiled at me. 'I had help from a certain Mr Lavender. Not his real name.'

'Mr who? Mr Lavender? Oh, is that the civilian you mentioned before?'

'Yes. He created a diversion. Thanks to him I was

able to disable the opposition and then go in to extract the team. Mr Gray was there, he admitted that he was the one who betrayed the team to the opposition. At one point he had me cold, but Mr Lavender rescued me, again. Mr Gray is now also disabled.'

'Nobody fainted?'

'Not by the time we had left. The local authorities were on their way, so I expect they will have made up some plausible story by now. Some story to explain why they were left tied up in their burning garden. Or in the house in Mr Gray's case.'

'Mr Gray will have been spirited away by now. Pity. We might have persuaded him to reveal the next link in the chain of traitors. I think this goes deep, Miss White, and it goes high perhaps to the top. How many of the opposition were there?'

'Four, including Mr Gray.'

'And you disabled them all, alone?'

'Mr Lavender and I.' She hesitated. 'We, we make a good team.' I gave her a big smile and a thumbs up.

'I see. Nonetheless, a civilian Miss White…' There was a long pause. 'Is he there now, your Mr Lavender?'

Elise looked at me. 'Yes, he's listening in.'

'Send him out for a moment. No, wait. Mr Lavender?'

'Erm, y-yes.' I replied.

'It seems we have something to thank you for. Tell Miss White to make a cup of tea or something.' Elise heard this, of course. Her face was a picture. I turned to her and winked before replying.

'I'm not sh-sure I dare!' There was a bark of laughter from the other end of the phone, quickly cut short. 'Nonetheless,' the voice continued, 'I wish to speak to you alone. It's important.'

Elise rolled her eyes and left the room. 'But I'm *not* making tea!' was her Parthian shot. The door closed behind her with a bang.

'Are we alone, Mr Lavender?'

'Yes.'

'Good. Now tell me about what happened. Where did you meet Miss White?'

'Um, in my b-bedroom. It was her final training mission. Sh-she was taking shelter from the Russians. She had been b-betrayed and had to run for it. My bedroom window was open; she didn't mean to disturb me, but...'

'I see. Then what happened?'

I told her the story. How we had managed to complete the mission by retrieving the coding machine, then about how Elise had been kidnapped, and finally how we had followed the leads to the house in London.

'I see.' Silence

'Erm, M-ma'am? What shall I call you? We've been calling you the boss lady.'

Again, a snort of laughter, quickly cut short. 'Call me Dr Gold. Well, Mr Lavender. You seem to have got involved in something here.'

'I d-do, don't I?'

'From what you have told me, I get the sense that, until the last, Miss White kept you out of sight?'

'Y-yes. She was trying to protect me. B-but now Mr Gray knows about me, b-but not who I am.'

'I see.'

'Please?'

'Yes.'

'P-please don't send me away from her.'

'Oh. *I see*... It's like that is it?' I kept quiet. 'And she?'

'I don't know. I *th-think* she likes me, but she likes Mr Plum as well.'

Silence again.

'Very well. Ask her to come in. Then *you* go and make a cup of tea!'

I left the room for the kitchen, and Elise took the phone. When she called me back in, after a few minutes, I tried to read her expression – desperate to find some hope in it. Her manner was grave, but there were no tears. I put two cups of tea on the coffee table.

'She told me I had to take you back home. But,' she added hastily, as she saw my face fall, 'I'm to keep in touch with you. You're to stay under the radar, and *I* can judge when to contact you.'

A huge grin spread across my face. I couldn't help it. She gave a happy little squeal. She crossed the room and launched herself at me like a red-tipped arrow. I was enfolded in an enthusiastic embrace, as I staggered back and fell down on the sofa.

She kissed me once on the lips, and then got up. 'Ahem. Well, we'd better see about getting you home, then. I'm to keep this house as my base and operate under the designation of Sigma One. That means I'm only eighteen miles away from you. I'm going to be busy for a while; we have to find the mole who betrayed us all.'

So that's what we did. I went home – with my new clothes and my new camping equipment. I told my parents that I had bought the camping stuff with my farming money, sharing the cost with Mike, since we would be going away together a fair amount. Explaining away my new clothes was more difficult, but by means of obfuscation, muttering about birthday money, and by outrageous lying, I managed to get away with it. Life settled back into its old, tedious routine and I discreetly threw away my old clothes.

— CHAPTER TWENTY-TWO —
Mr Plum in a Stew

October came along and the weather turned colder. The trees in Dokesley woods were clothed in the colours of burnished copper and bronze, and fiery red. I loved autumn. I have always thought it the most beautiful time of the year.

I walked – and ran – in the woods a lot those first few weeks without Elise. I thought of her all the time, but I thought of her particularly, every time I jogged past the turning tree over the river. I smiled each time at the thought of the Russian agent floundering about in the water.

Elise had popped back once, briefly, one Sunday in September. I introduced her to my parents as a 'friend', but I think my mother at least guessed there might be more to it than that. Elise was on her best behaviour that day; she was not at all sarcastic or judgemental. I could only imagine the effort that must have cost her.

We went for a walk in the woods away from prying eyes and ears. She told me how things were going. Not well, I gathered. Mr Plum was recovering in a 'government facility' and there was no sign of the mole, who seemed to have done what moles do, and gone underground. She was upset because she had not been allowed to see Mr Plum.

'He's in a kind of quarantine,' she fretted.

My heart sank. She still had feelings for him, that was clear.

She was still living in Doncaster at the safe house, although how long it would remain safe was anybody's guess. The teenage trainees were still grounded, and safe in the house at Hertford. I was back at school, which seemed very boring after the excitement of the Summer. I even started to do essays and revision. I was so bored!

Dr Gold was running things from wherever she had taken shelter. Elise was in touch with her by phone, at the safe house in Doncaster.

Elise, too, was grounded, at least at first. This did not suit her restless personality, and after many protests and much pleading, she obtained permission to call on me a bit more often. She had quite a few more family meals with us, and she sometimes volunteered to do the washing up, which endeared her to my mother no end. They were soon firm friends, and I could hear the two of them in the kitchen. There was much laughter. I could guess what they were laughing at, or rather, who!

*

One day, at the start of the half-term holiday, Elise turned up at the house, and we went for a walk in Dokesley woods. I showed her the turning tree. We walked arm in arm, but the weather wasn't the only thing that was chilly. She seemed distant, distracted even. She perked up a bit when we got to the tree and I described the man falling into the river in great, and hilarious detail, but I could tell there was something not right. I couldn't bear it, I had to know what had changed.

'Elise, have I d-done s-something wrong?'

I looked at her and was confronted by a horror-stricken face.

'No, no, of course not! Oh, Phil-Will.' She hugged me and held me tight. I was reminded of just how strong she was, as her arms fastened round me in a powerful hug. On a hug-ometer it was more like a wild grizzly bear than Gentle Ben. I had difficulty breathing for a moment, but I hugged her back. She gave me a tender kiss on the lips.

'Phil, I'm scared. Something's happened, but I'm not supposed to tell you.'

'Scared? *You*?' I was amazed. In all our adventures she had been afraid of nothing, while I had been terrified the whole time! Excited, yes, loved-up, yes, but also very terrified. My legs still turned weak when I remembered some of the things we had done, and I still had bad dreams. In spite of this I was ready to do it all again, if it meant that I could be by Elise's side.

'Yes, scared. I get scared too you know!'

I was taken aback by the vehemence of her reply. 'Well, you're v-very good at not sh-showing it.'

'Oh, now I've made you stutter. I'm sorry, I didn't mean to snap at you. Look, if I tell you will you promise me not to mention it to a living soul?'

'Who would b-believe me anyway?'

'Good point! Well. In spite of all the precautions and the security they've… they've got hold of Mr Plum again.' Tears were rolling down her cheek, and her voice became a squeak. 'And I know they're going to kill him this time.'

I took her in my arms and held her tight. She sobbed into my shoulder. I had never seen her like this, it upset me greatly. She must really love him. My heart went down into my boots. I had stood little chance with this beautiful and enigmatic girl before, but now that the man she hero-worshipped was in serious trouble, I had no chance at all. He was her hero, her mentor and he held her heart – and now he needed her as he never had done before.

I swallowed. Then I did the hardest thing I had ever done in my life. Nothing, not even in all our adventures together, compared with the difficulty of what I did at this point. I looked her in the eye, and I smiled. She returned my gaze, looking up at me, with her tear-stained, trusting, beautiful face and my heart did somersaults all over again.

I cleared my throat. 'Well,' I decided. 'We'd better

find him, and get him back, hadn't we 007?'

She blew her nose on an inadequate looking hanky. She gave a gulp and blinked back her tears.

'Oh, Phil,' she murmured. 'I knew you'd have a plan. I didn't know what to do, but then I thought "Phil will have a plan".'

Actually, Phil had no plan at all! But being with Elise seemed to stimulate my brain, so I suggested we should sit down and think things through together. We walked back to my house. Luckily, both of my parents were out at work, so we could talk freely.

I made her tea and we sat down at the dining table.

'It happened two nights ago,' she began. 'Apparently there was some kind of celebration going on – a birthday or something. Everyone was in the main hall celebrating, and security was left to a skeleton crew of agents. Someone knocked out the agent who was guarding Mr Plum, and they must have taken him away. We still don't know how it happened, although I suppose I'd be the last to know, you know, for security reasons. Dr Gold told me about it, but she wasn't happy that I should know. She only gave me the barest information. She, she knew how much I… I admired him; so, she told me the news…' She finished with tears in her eyes. 'I don't think she was supposed to pass it on.'

'No one will find out from me,' I declared stoutly.

'Thanks, Phil.' She smiled at me. 'What would I have done without you?'

'You'll never have to do without me,' I replied, romantically.

She came around the table and gave me a kiss. Then she sat on my knee. I put my arms round her and she snuggled into my shoulder.

'What are we going to do, Phil-Will?' she asked.

What indeed.

'If they've got him out of the country, there's nothing we *can* do,' I muttered, thinking aloud.

'But I don't think they have. The service is watching all the ports and things,' she remembered.

We sat in silence a bit more, both of us in deep thought, and in deep feelings too. 'What about those two *visa-parsley domes*?' I said. 'The one in Sheffield and the one in Hornsey?'

She frowned. 'The…? Oh, you mean the *безопасныедома*? The safe houses?' I nodded. 'They're a no go, they won't use those again; they know we know about them. Oh. But. Wait a minute.' She jumped up from my lap, went to the front door, opened it and ran out to her car, hair streaming out behind her in the cool autumn wind.

She came back, smiling, her eyes sparkling, and her cheeks flushed with hope. She was holding some papers. She waved them at me and declared. 'Phil, you're a genius!'

She stood impatiently while I cleared the tea things from the table, then she deposited the papers on the cloth.

She sat down and riffled frantically through them.

'I'm sure I saw…back when we were in Doncaster and you were buying me clothes… Yes! Here…' She held up some pieces of paper, printed in Russian, with her scrawled translation all over them. She gave them to me.

They looked similar to the piece of paper that led us to Hornsey. I shrugged, puzzled.

'It's a list of expenses for different *безопасныедома*,' she explained. 'Look, this one's in Westmoreland. (The county of Westmoreland no longer exists, that area is now part of the county of Cumbria.) 'In Kendal. Shap Road. That's not too far from Scotland…'

'Where Mr Gray was,' I said. She nodded and looked at me with a pleading look.

'Well, it's somewhere to start, what are we waiting for?' I enthused. She threw her arms around me, giving me the biggest hug ever.

She spoke gently into my ear as she held me tight. 'I do know, you know. I do understand. I'm so grateful for your patience, Phil. Be patient with me a little longer. I can't get my head straight while he's in danger.'

I didn't know what to say. Tears started in my eyes and then rolled down my cheeks. I looked at her; then hugged her again, temporarily speechless. She pulled away.

'Well come on, *tempus fugit*, you know.' She blew her nose again.

— CHAPTER TWENTY-THREE —
Search for a Lost Love

We were back in the Mini and heading due north for Kendal. We followed the A1 for over a hundred miles. Elise drove like a demon. We covered the distance to Scotch Corner in an hour and a half, while I hung on for grim death. From there it was less than fifty miles along the A66 to Kendal, which she did in less than an hour. We had set off just after ten o'clock, we were in Kendal by half past twelve. It was an unseasonably warm afternoon, with bright autumnal sunshine, and no wind.

'Lunch?' asked my ever-hungry companion. 'We can't go hunting on an empty stomach. And we need a council of war!'

We found a small restaurant. It was designed for the tourists who came to see the Lake District, so it was on the expensive side, but Elise still had her expense account, so she didn't really care. We ordered a meal. I went for fish and chips – it was called something more posh than that, but that's really what it was. Elise tried the beef bourguignon.

Then we put our heads together over coffee.

'I don't think we can do the fire thing again, Phil-Will!' She smiled. 'They'll be wise to that this time.'

'Why don't we "case the joint" to start with?' I replied. 'Then we might see some sort of a way in.'

'Or we might see that it's impossible. Or that there's no one there after all.' She sighed. 'Phil, I can't help feeling our luck is going to run out sometime. It's been a crazy, impossible adventure, and I couldn't live with myself if something happened to you.'

I took her hands. 'And if something happened to Mr P-Plum? Oh heavens, what is his real n-name. I c-can't keep calling him Mr Plum!'

She gave a sad smile. 'It's Ken. Short for Kendrick. Look, I don't want anything to happen to him, either, but with you I feel responsible. I got you into this.'

'And I k-kept me in it. I could have p-pulled out at any time.'

'Really? With the way you're feeling?'

So, she understood! I looked down, then back up again. I looked straight into those anxious, teary eyes. 'It's still a ch-choice,' I heard myself saying. 'I ch-choose to be with you, to g-go with you, to the end... and... and if that is seeing you r-ride off into the sunset in your mini with K-Ken, then...Well, then that's the way it has to be. Oh, Elise. I was terrified the whole t-time, I was literally scared sick, and I still have n-nightmares about what we went through in the summer, but honestly? I wouldn't ch-change a thing. You've shown me a side of me I didn't know existed. You wondered about what talents I might have, I never thought of me as having any talents at all until you came along. And then there's the fact that…' I paused and hung my head, looking at her was so difficult at this moment.

'Yes?' she asked, encouragingly, taking my hand. 'The fact that…?'

'The f-fact that you've roused feelings in me I d-didn't know I was capable of. If anyone t-tells me I don't know anything about love, I c-can laugh in their face now!' A fugitive tear escaped from my right eye and rolled down my cheek.

She leaned forward across the table, pulled me to her and nestled her damp cheek against mine. Tears coursed freely down both our faces and mingled so that it was impossible to tell who was crying more.

'Oh, Phil.' She sighed. 'I don't know what to say…'

'S-Say something s-sarky, for g-goodness sake,' I sniffed.

I felt her face next to mine shake, as she laughed through her tears.

'Are you going to eat those chips?'

We had navigated a difficult moment and had come through it, still friends. But my heart ached. Why did love hurt so much?

Elise was speaking, I re-focused. '…I'll just be glad if we come out of it with our lives!' She finished, while she polished off my last few, cold, chips. 'All right, plan boy, what now?'

She was impatient to get going, I understood why. The man she had first set her heart on was in serious trouble. We were his only hope.

I thought. And what I thought was, *we need binoculars!* So that was decided upon. In the Lake District there were outdoor type shops around every corner. Millets had to compete with a good many other outdoor stores, both large and small, in this town on the edge of the national park. Elise bought two pairs, identical models for each of us, and stowed them in the backpack she had brought with her from the car. She heaved the heavy-looking pack onto her back, and we set off. I knew better than to offer to carry it for her!

Armed with a street map of Kendal, we made our way towards the address of the safe house. We left the Mini some way back, and we finished the journey on foot. We walked along the road almost out of Kendal altogether. Like the Sheffield house, this one was on the edge of town. It was a large, detached house in its own grounds, with gates across a drive. If the Russians really were based here, it must be their main headquarters. How many people would be in there? The walls were high and topped with spikes. It looked almost like a fortress. My heart sank. I could think of no way to get in there.

Opposite the house, meadows ran down to the river. I was half hoping that the house would be deserted. I was getting the familiar weak feeling in my legs, and I was breathing heavily, as if I'd been running.

We acted like tourists; we walked through the meadow and down to the river, hand in hand. Beside a clump of willows, we settled down into the grass, as if we were there for a snog – despite the cool weather. Elise gave me the bag to hold for a moment, while she reached into it for the binoculars. I almost collapsed; it was really heavy!

'What on earth have you got in here?' I said with a gasp. Elise didn't reply, but she rummaged in the bag and produced the binoculars. She handed me a pair.

'Hey, these are amazing!' I could see the house clearly; the distance was about a hundred and fifty yards (not metres in those days!) and I could make out just about every brick.

'I got military standard ones,' Elise muttered distractedly, intently scrutinising the house through her own set of binoculars. 'They have non-reflective lenses.'

'Why?'

'It means they won't see us looking at them, ninny!'

'Oh. Yes. Of course. Ha-ha!' I said. 'By the way, welcome back, Sarky One, I've missed you!'

She gave a wry smile, leaned across and ruffled my hair.

'And goodbye stutter!' she said. She focused on the house again. 'I can hardly see anything, what with the wall, and a solid steel gate, it's impossible. Wait, there's a car!' She said excitedly. I could see it; a car was drawing up to the house in front of the driveway. 'It's not deserted! At least that's something.' Her mood changed. Suddenly she was all professional again. It was remarkable to watch. Her features hardened; her expression changed. She became calm, ice-cold, in fact. 'I won't need to actually shoot anyone unless they resist.' She remarked casually. Then, with more vehemence, 'But I hope they resist, oh please let them resist!' She pulled a second gun from her backpack and checked it over.

'Here,' she added. 'I have one for you as well.'

'But I've never used a gun. If I shoot it, I'm just as likely to hit you as anything else!'

'Take it for now. Maybe you won't have to use it, except perhaps to threaten someone.'

As I slipped the gun into my pocket, it gave me the glimmerings of an idea, a desperate idea, but this was a desperate situation. They might be torturing Ken in that house this very minute.

But first, I was curious. 'Why haven't your people arrested these guys?'

'Until we find the mole everything has come to a grinding halt. But now Mr… now Ken has been taken, it's different. Suddenly it's panic stations. He knows too much. Everything's got up to full speed again. People are searching for him night and day. I would contact someone and get them here, but I just don't know who to trust now. We are watching all entry and exit points, so it will be difficult for them to get him out. I expect that's why they are lying low here. I'm really afraid for him; they might find it easier just to kill him, if they haven't already.' Elise's face was grim, but her lip trembled as she spoke. I felt compelled to try and encourage her.

'I bet he's too valuable to them,' I reassured. 'They'll try and get him back to Russia and give him truth drugs and stuff.'

'Truth drugs? They're no good. You just say what you think the interrogator wants to hear. No.' Her voice trembled. 'They'll just beat him until he can't stand the pain any longer, or...'

'Or?'

'Or, he dies.' She released the safety catch on the gun. I did the same. I wasn't going to make that mistake again.

While we were speaking, the formidable steel gates had opened, the car drove in as we watched, then the gates swung slowly to again. But not before we got a good look inside. Elise's eyes were riveted on the house though her binoculars.

'Big garden at the front,' she murmured. 'Lots of trees for cover.'

I focused on what I could see of the garden as the gates slowly swung to. She was right. There was a longish drive, through a landscaped garden with a good number of trees. My plan was becoming more solid in my mind all the time.

'And a sentry patrolling the grounds,' Elise remarked. 'So, what's the plan, Phil? I don't see any rubbish lying around for making a fire!'

I smiled, but she was serious.

'I still think we'll do better at night,' I replied. A plan was beginning to form in my mind. It was crazy, but what the hey, all my plans so far had been crazy. 'So, we've got two guns,' I said thoughtfully.

'No, I brought four,' she replied. 'One for each of our hands'

'Four?' I squeaked.

'Yes. Three from the three heavies in London, and one from Mr Gray. Well, you never know when one's going to jam, and it gives you twice the ammunition before you have to reload!'

'I think you just like having them!'

She blushed, smiled mischievously, looked at me and shrugged. 'I picked up lots of ammunition from that house in Hornsey when I was looking for the keys to open that cellar door. It was all in a cupboard, so I took it.'

'I thought you were a long time, I assumed you'd been rummaging around for the keys all that time! Oh well, anyway, it's good. The more noise we can make, the better,' I declared.

'Ah, another diversion,' she gushed. 'Not with a fire, but with fire*power*!'

'Teach me to shoot, at least in the general direction I want.'

'We only have a couple of hours before it gets dark.'

'Well, we have to do something for the next couple of hours!'

There was silence for a moment. She was looking at me with that raised eyebrow, and that wry look I had seen before. 'And you want to use the time by learning to shoot? Figures!' And she sighed.

— CHAPTER TWENTY-FOUR —
Lost Love Found

We walked further out of town, right out into the countryside, to a deserted spot on the river. No one would be disturbed by shots out here. She placed a large stone on the branch of a tree, in the crook, where it joined the trunk.

'OK, this is how it works.' She put the gun in my hand and stood next to me. 'Grip the gun high on the back strap. You need to control the recoil. Hold the gun like this,' and she arranged my hands on the weapon. I was distracted for a moment by the smooth softness of her hands on mine. I tried to re-focus.

'Both your hands should fit together, like this,' she continued. 'That's good. Now. Extend both of your arms forward and raise the gun to eye-level, so you can see your sights *and* the target. No, not like that! I'm surprised My Gray didn't die laughing! Bend your elbows slightly, they shouldn't be fully locked – I told you, you need to absorb the recoil! OK, there's the target in the tree there. It's a fat partridge and you're hungry. Line the front sight with your two rear sights. Focus on placing the front sight on the target. It's impossible to keep everything in focus, so your target will be a bit blurred. However, your front sight should be crystal clear. Now take your trigger finger off the guard and feel the trigger. No, don't look! I said *feel* it. Better! Now, remember I told you this is a Makarov, the first shot will take the most effort. When you've fired the first one, fire two more straight away.'

I squeezed the trigger, and squeezed, and squeezed. Eventually the gun went off, taking me by surprise. In spite of her warnings, I wasn't ready for the recoil and the shot went almost straight up into the air.'

'Go on,' said my relentless teacher. 'Fire two more straight away.'

I did and this time it was easier. It went better. At least the bullets went in the general direction of the tree.

Elise had turned away. I thought she was showing disgust, but as she turned back, I could see she had been laughing. 'Go on,' she said. 'I have plenty of ammunition, empty the magazine. Try and hit *something* over in that general direction!'

So that was why the rucksack was so heavy, four guns and all that ammunition, I thought to myself.

Then I concentrated on what I was supposed to be doing.

By now I was cross, both with myself, and with her sarcasm. I was determined to wipe that laugh off her face! I thought about everything she had told me, and I fired off three shots in rapid succession. She was right, after the first big effort, emptying the gun was much easier. I hit the tree, then I hit the stone twice in succession, with the satisfying sound of two ricochets. Her face was a picture.

She didn't speak for a moment. 'Well, either I'm a superb teacher or you're just a natural.'

'I think it's your teaching, I just thought carefully about everything you said, plus you made me mad.'

'Maybe it's both. Well, whatever it is, I think you've got it.'

She showed me how to reload, and empty, the gun a few times; then I reloaded it and tried another gun-full of bullets. I hit the stone four times out of six. We didn't want to use up precious ammo, so we stopped at that point.

'Twelve shots, five on target,' she said approvingly. 'Not bad, not bad at all.' She hugged me. Then she said, 'Come on, I'm hungry.'

We retraced our steps back to the car, it was quite a walk, and we had gone a long way out of town. We found somewhere to have an early dinner, and while we ate, darkness began to fall. Elise once again tucked into her food with a will, but I couldn't eat much, my stomach was filled with butterflies.

'Aren't you going to finish that?' she asked, after clearing her plate in no time.

I shook my head and pushed it across to her.

'I didn't like the look of those spikes on the wall. I think there might be broken glass up there as well.' Opined Elise casually, as she finished my meal.

I thought hard. 'We need rope,' I decided.

'Easy,' she remarked, her mouth full of my food.

'All those outdoor shops: rope, lots, mountaineers for the use of.'

We formulated a plan. Once again, she left me in a pub, while she went off to make the purchases. I sipped my Coke and worried. She came back with the rope, a second rucksack for me, two balaclavas and some boot polish.

When she came back, she got herself a Coke too. 'No wine?' I teased.

Her face was absolutely serious, as she replied: 'Not before a mission, Phil-Will.' Then her face cracked briefly into a smile. 'Besides, if you have a glass of wine, you'll shoot anything that moves, including me!' It wasn't very funny, but we both laughed.

I held up my glass. 'Here's to a successful mission, and to…to Ken.' I almost choked on the words, but I got them out. Elise held up her glass. 'To a successful mission,' she said, pointedly.

By now it was six o'clock and completely dark. We spent some time sitting in the Mini working on the rope, adapting it to our needs. Elise's skill in knot making was remarkable; she was so quick and deft. She made foot-loops in the rope. She then divided up the guns and ammunition between us. We put the boot polish on our faces to darken them and donned the balaclavas.

Elise drove us to a road from where we could approach the back of the house. She left the Mini where it wouldn't be seen by anyone inside. We were wearing dark clothes and with the balaclavas and darkened faces, we were like wraiths in the night. We left the car some distance away and, starting round the back of the safe house, we did a full reconnoitre of the place. Our backpacks were filled with guns, ammunition and the rope. We had the binoculars slung around our necks. The mood was sombre. We both realised how dangerous this was going to be.

'Just so you know, I've never shot anyone. Only targets,' said my trigger-happy companion.

'Really?'

'Really. But I was really good at that.' She winked.

'Remember you're supposed to be aiming to disable them,' I warned her.

She wriggled a little. 'OK, but if they've hurt Ken… Well, I won't be answerable! Anyway, what will you be aiming for?'

'The sky!'

We went on through the darkness of the cool October night, and finished our circuit of the house.

'That might be a problem,' she hissed, pointing to two floodlights on the front of the building, 'There's one at the back too. That's where the first shots go, then,' she murmured, half to herself. 'I'd better do that. But how many do you think there are in the house?'

'It's impossible to tell for sure, but according to your translation, they aren't eating any more bread than the other safe houses,' I remembered. 'I guess we'll find out once the shooting starts,' I added wryly.

'Come on!' she exclaimed, and I followed her at the run, following the wall to the front gate. 'Your turn to get down.' She made me get down on my hands and knees and stood on my back. She cautiously peeped over the top of the gate.

After a minute or two – it seemed a lot longer with her size four boots on my back – she jumped down and crouched beside me to hiss at me.' There are two guards, one patrolling the front, one the back. I'm going to need to watch them for a bit. Will you be OK?'

I smiled through my pain. 'If it takes all summer, general,' I said, quoting the American civil war General, Ulysses Grant.

Elise smiled back. 'That's the spirit,' she said and rubbed my back. It helped. She climbed back up again.

She timed the guards, then jumped down and crouched next to me again, rubbing my back as she spoke. 'They patrol the length of the house, and back again, which brings them back face-to-face, they have a brief chat round the front here, before starting back. They're very consistent,' she murmured in my ear. 'They are taking exactly four minutes in between chats.'

'We can get over the back wall, while they're round the front.' She nodded without replying, still massaging my back. I bit my lip.

She looked at me. 'You OK?' she asked anxiously, noting the expression on my face.

Now that it was all about to kick off, I was being afflicted by a fear bordering on terror. People would soon be shooting at us. I felt a sudden knot in my stomach. My mouth became dry. I didn't want to get up from this crouch because I wasn't sure that my legs would hold me up.

There was no point in being anything but honest, she must be able to see I was struggling. 'Elise,' I said, in a sort of dry, quavering croak. 'How do you handle the nerves? Right now, I feel so scared that I want to run away!'

She must have felt like Wellington would have if all his generals had chickened out before the battle of Waterloo. In spite of this she looked at me with nothing but compassion in her eyes. She put down the backpack and there, under the shadow of the formidable wall of the fortified house, she took me in her arms and rocked me, as if we had all the time in the world, as if the man she loved was not being tortured somewhere in the building behind that wall.

If I'd loved her before, I loved her even more now. Tears ran down my cheeks, I couldn't help it.

'Oh, Phil-Will,' she murmured with sympathy in her voice and tears in her eyes. 'You've done so well. I sometimes forget you're not trained for this. Look, why don't you wait in the car. You can be the getaway driver? We might need to get out of here fast.'

I took several deep, ragged breaths. I thought about it. Could I, perhaps, possibly let her go through this on her own? My love for Elise fought against the fear, a war in my insides. Love won. The thought of Elise, hurt, captured or, oh dear heaven, dead…and my fault? Not to be borne.

'No, no, just give me a minute.' I croaked through parched lips. 'We need as many guns as possible for the plan.'

She looked deep into my eyes as I stared at her through my tears. I wiped them away and gave her a smile. She nodded, as if satisfied with what she saw.

'Attaboy!' She pulled me up. She looked at her watch. 'It's a four-minute cycle remember.'

I followed her lead as we scurried around the back of the house. Elise was looking at her illuminated watch as she ran and counted under her breath. We stopped under the ten-foot-high wall. She was still counting off the seconds.

'Now,' she hissed. The two men would be at the front of the house having a little natter. As luck would have it, they had decided to light up for a quick smoke as well, giving us a few more precious seconds. We threw a big loop of the rope up, so that it lassoed three of the metal spikes. Holding the two strands of rope Elise swarmed to the top of the wall, aided by foot-loops she had tied earlier. I scrambled up after her. She was right about the broken glass; it was cemented to the top of the wall, lethally sharp. We balanced precariously ten feet above the ground, clinging to the spikes.

'Fifteen seconds!' she hissed. She threw down the ropes and we scrambled down the other side of the wall. Elise pulled on one end of the double strand of rope, and it came down, falling in loose coils round our feet. Elise rapidly stowed it. The house was lit with the three floodlights, two at the front and one at the back. The only shadow was against the house, right underneath the light. We ran for it. We paused, hidden in the pool of shade. The house itself seemed in darkness, all the curtains were drawn; it must have been blackout material, because barely a chink of light escaped.

My heart was pounding, uncomfortably high in my throat, adrenalin was causing all my limbs to shake, and as for shooting, I didn't think I was going to be able to pull the trigger, let alone hit anything!

We each took a fully loaded gun in each hand. Elise gave me half of the boxes of ammunition from her backpack, and I put them into mine.

'OK, for luck,' she babbled and grabbed me, giving

me a big kiss on the lips. Then she was away. If my head was spinning before, it was whirling now.

We separated according to the plan we had made. She ran for the side of the house at the opposite end to the two guards. I stayed where I was for a moment. The plan was for Elise to fire off seven or eight shots, before I joined in, then she would reload while I was still firing, and vice versa. The idea was to make them think they were being raided by a small platoon.

I was startled by the sudden noise as she gave a high-pitched yell, and her gun crashed out in the silent night, sounding like the ending of the world. At the first shot the floodlight went out, and the backyard was in darkness. As the guards ran around to the back she was dashing to the front, firing indiscriminately, then taking out the floodlights at the front. The two guards spun around and raced back towards the front of the house. Eight shots in all rang out; then I screamed and started firing towards the two men, but over their heads. They dived for cover around the side of the house. I reloaded, crouching down in the darkness. Elise had kept on running round and was now sneaking up behind the two guards, who were pinned down by my wildly indiscriminate shooting.

From close behind one of the guards, Elise's gun fired twice. One of the men turned and ran towards her, then I fired from the opposite direction, just behind the other guard. Each guard fired back. In the dark and confusion, we now had them shooting at each other. We kept running, shouting and shooting. Elise at the front, and I at the back. The guards alternately shot at us and at each other.

It was total bedlam. I was high on adrenalin. I crouched down by the side of the house and took the opportunity to reload. 'Good shooting,' whispered a voice in my ear. I almost leapt right out of my skin, like Tom and Jerry on the telly. It was Elise, of course.

'Come on,' she panted. We sprinted round to the front and headed for the trees. 'You go, over there, you're faster than me. Crossfire.' She pointed to the trees by the drive, near the other side of the building. We crouched in the shadows, one at either end of the building, unseen but with a good view of the front door, and fired at the guards, who by now were crouching one either side of the building and firing back at us. After a while they stopped, they must have run out of ammunition, they would not have been expecting a full-scale battle! I hadn't realised it, but Elise had worked this out.

The big wooden front door began to open cautiously, and Elise emptied one of her guns into it. I heard the bullets smacking into the wood, and the door slammed shut immediately. She continued with the plan, running from tree to tree, firing off shots, as if there were several of her, I did the same. She zigged and I zagged.

Light suddenly blazed out. Someone opened a window upstairs and began firing into the dark night, aiming towards where we had been a moment before, a machine pistol by the sound of it – I recognised it from the films I watched. This was a dangerous moment. Elise never flinched, she coolly took aim, and as the arm appeared again to shoot blindly into the shadows, she fired. There was a howl of pain and the arm was withdrawn. Someone had the idea of opening the curtains downstairs so as to shed some light on whoever was shooting at them. Elise immediately shattered the window with three or four bullets, and the curtains were hurriedly drawn to again.

'Keep firing,' she yelled. I obeyed. I had a fine time shooting at all the windows. I started to get cocky and began firing each gun in turn, like Clint Eastwood in *A Fistful of Dollars*. It must have been hell in that house, with bullets coming through the widows, flying all round the room, windows smashing, lethal shards of glass whistling through the air. I was running low on ammunition and just beginning to get a knot in my stomach, wondering how we would pull this off if we ran out of bullets, when someone poked a walking stick through a broken window upstairs, with a white handkerchief on the end.

'Disappear,' she hissed at me, still trying to protect me. Even at this stage she was still trying to keep my identity hidden. I considered protesting, but I thought better of it.

'*выйти с вашимируками вверх*!' yelled Elise at the top of her voice. (Come out with your hands up!) One by one four men emerged from the house with their hands up. Someone must have contacted the two guards by walkie-talkie; they came round to surrender as well. One of them was helping his companion, whom he had shot and wounded in the leg, by mistake.

'никакихтрюков, моилюдисмотрят,' Elise said. (No tricks, my men are watching.) She disarmed them and made them lie face down on the driveway. She got some lengths of rope out of the seemingly bottomless rucksack, and tied their hands behind their backs, and their legs together.

She turned in my direction and yelled, 'Stay there everybody. Keep your guns trained on these thugs, if they move, shoot them. I'm going into the house.' The adrenalin was still shooting through my veins, it was impossible to make myself understand for a moment that it was over. When I did, I wanted to laugh. *'Everybody?'* I put my guns away, one in my waistband in approved movie style and one in my pocket.

CHAPTER TWENTY-FIVE

Love and Mr Plum

Elise disappeared into the house. I took up a position in the garden. The night was unnaturally still and quiet after all that noise. I sank down to a sitting position behind a tree in deep shadow. I peeped through the foliage. I saw she had made her way upstairs as she now opened the curtains in one of the front bedrooms on the first floor and waved briefly at me. I guessed she had found Mr Plum. She turned away from the window. She disappeared from view as if she was bending over a bed.

There was a lull for some time. Once again, as in Hornsey, I began to be impatient. I could wait no longer. I yelled out, to the imaginary platoon. 'I'm going in, stay here men and watch them.'

I strolled over towards the house, looking forward to receiving the thanks of the precious prisoner, and a big hug from Elise. I paused. Or would she be so taken up with *him*, that I wouldn't even get a look-in, let alone a hug? The fear grew in me that they would be enjoying a quiet snog, while I kicked my heels outside. The green monster inside me roared. I walked more quickly, pushed open the door, desperate now to end this gnawing uncertainty.

I got no further than the bottom of the stairs. Elise was on her way down, but not voluntarily. An arm was around her throat, and she was being pushed along, ahead of a man whom I had seen before. I was struck dumb. It was Mr Plum! I almost didn't recognise him without all the bruises. His right arm was round her throat and his right hand held a knife to the jugular vein in her neck, his left hand was behind her, and I guessed he also had a gun. We all stood, frozen in a sort of tableau. It took me a moment to understand it. Mr Plum, the man we had risked our lives to save, was now holding a gun and a knife to his rescuer...the girl who adored him. Elise had removed her balaclava; her blackened face did not look adoring at this moment. I had never seen her look so angry in all our brief acquaintance, and the tears streaming down her face did nothing to soften her expression.

'Well, well, is that *Mr Lavender* under there; I presume?' sneered the former Sigma One. I assumed he was guessing; he couldn't see my face. I stood frozen in shock and said nothing.

'You move, and she dies,' he declared. I had only heard him say two sentences, but already his voice was beginning to grate on me.

'Don't mind me, shoot him!' snarled a voice I barely

recognised, so full of anger and venom.

'Not as long as I might hit you, Sigma One,' I breathed. My heart rate must have been at record levels, higher than it had been even during the gun battle outside. I tried to think quickly, to put aside my shock and the fact that the girl I loved was in such severe peril, and to find a way out of this mess. Nothing came to me. I could see no way out.

'Sigma One is *my* designation!' he snarled. 'As far as the world is concerned, I will be Sigma One again.' His voice became smarmier. 'How well you did, Elise, my darling, dealing with all those agents, practically by yourself. Your plan? No, surely not. His plan, yes, I bet. You were always too impetuous, my love, rushing in instead of standing back, to take time to think. Well, it's really got you in hot water this time. When I've dealt with the two of you, I'll be the only one left to tell the story of how you rescued me, but then fell to a stray bullet, just as we were on the point of escaping. I dealt with the shooter, but not before you died in my arms! What a tragedy. They'll award you both posthumous medals.'

I finally found my voice. 'Our men are outside.' I bluffed. 'You can't get away; the place is surrounded. Better for you if you surrender now.'

'It's no good, Ph...Mr Lavender. I told him everything; before...' Elise sounded miserable. For the first time since I had met her, she sounded, well, defeated.

'Before I grabbed her,' smirked the traitor.

'To think I kissed you! I admired you so much, and, and you betrayed us all.' Elise was sobbing and almost incoherent in her anger.

'Yes, I realised you had a crush on me from early on in training. I encouraged you. I thought it might be nice to have a little training affair! It was quite useful really, as it turned out. I never thought anyone would find me at this safe house, so it was a real shock for all of us, when the shooting started. You shouldn't have shouted; I recognised your voice. I guessed you two were working alone, like before. I told my colleagues to surrender; I told them I would make sure that they were released sometime down the line. I went upstairs to my room and pretended to be tied up. It amused me to think I was being "rescued" by a lovesick girl. OK, throw your weapon on the floor!'

So, she hadn't told him *absolutely* everything! I gave Elise a look. Her head came up, and her eyes filled once more with hope. I smiled at her.

'Chin up, Sarky One,' I gushed. She smiled back.

'Less talking and more action! Drop that gun on the floor now… slowly!' I took the gun from my pocket and dropped it as ordered.

'Kick it away!' I kicked the gun, and sent it skidding across the tiled floor. 'Now put your hands up,' he growled. I obeyed. 'Now go outside.' His voice was becoming complacent. He felt he had the situation well under control.

I had never felt so angry. I felt it rise like a tide inside me. It made me feel defiant.

'Why?' I asked. I was still terrified, but now I was super-angry as well, and that was keeping my mind working.

'What?'

'Well, if you're going to shoot us and make it look as though we were killed out there, why should we help you?'

This had always puzzled me about films. Why did the victim always do what the villain wanted? If they wanted to shoot you in a certain place, why walk there like a lamb to the slaughter? Why make life easy for the murderer? I decided to make life difficult at least for this particular villain. I folded my arms.

'Get your hands up and move, or I shoot her!'

Elise joined in. 'He's got a point, Ken. We should at least make you carry our bodies outside.'

While he was distracted, I slowly moved my folded arms down towards my waist and the hidden gun.

'Fine, I'll shoot you here, starting with you!' And he threw Elise to one side so as to have both hands free and aimed the gun at me. As he threw her down, I dived desperately for the floor. His gun cracked, and a bullet went just over my head. I grabbed for my gun and got it free of my clothes, but before I could do anything there was another crack!

I don't know if you've ever been in an accident, or seen one happen. Your brain goes into emergency mode and everything seems to happen in slow motion. This was happening now, as I lay on the floor panting; a quick internal check revealed no especial pain. I was not hit. Then I looked up at Ken, still holding the gun. His eyes were wide open in shock, and he was clutching his leg. He'd been shot. Had he shot himself by accident? Had my gun gone off by accident? I looked beyond him. Elise was on her knees, her smoking gun pointing at Ken. We were all frozen as in a photograph. Then normal time returned, Ken's surprised yell of pain rang out, blood seeped through his fingers as he held his thigh, staggered and fell onto one knee. He raised his gun towards me, only to see I was pointing my gun at his head. With a heartfelt cry of angry defeat, he threw down his gun and put up his hands. It was over. It was really over. As always, Elise reacted fastest. She approached Ken, still pointing her gun at him. He had thrown her to the floor right next to my gun, the one I had surrendered; and she had made the most of the opportunity.

'Lie down, hands behind your back,' she snarled. Angry wasn't the word for her current mood, ferocious would be nearer.

'Mr Lavender, the rope. Upstairs, bedroom on the left.'

I ran, fuelled by adrenalin, I took the stairs two and three at a time. Giddy with relief, I grabbed her bag from the bed in the bedroom and came back as quick as I could. I reached into it and passed Elise some rope.

I kept my gun trained on Ken and made sure he could see it. She tied him up. She wasn't gentle. This man had encouraged her to have feelings for him, then he had exploited them. Finally, he had betrayed everything she thought he stood for, including her, and her love for him. Tears still streamed down her face while she worked. When she was done, she stood up, and wiped her tears away with her sleeve, smearing the boot polish all over her face.

When she had tied his hands securely behind his back, she removed his belt and undid his trousers. For a moment I thought she was going to take the belt to him and deal out some corporal punishment. I would not have blamed her, although I would have tried to stop her... probably. But that wasn't it. She pulled his trousers down to access the bleeding wound in his leg.

'Mr Lavender, there's a first aid box in the kitchen.'

She was being thoroughly professional. I tried to come up to her standards. 'Very well, *Sigma One*' I emphasised the last two words just to rub salt into his wounds.

With the first aid box Elise was able to apply a bandage and stop the bleeding.

'Don't tell me...you learned first aid in the girl guides!' I quipped. She smiled for the first time in quite a while.

'How did you guess?' She gave me that 'didn't he do well' look, the one that always made me feel like wagging my tail. Then she launched herself at me and hugged me half to death.

'What made you come in this time? You were suspicious of him, weren't you?' She looked me in the eye. 'Be honest, you knew. How did you know?'

Oh, it was so tempting. I would have looked really cool if I had told her I suspected him from the start, but with her looking at me like that, I just couldn't lie.

'You want to know the truth?' She nodded eagerly. 'I had an attack of jealousy. I thought you two might be up there snogging, while I was outside. I'm sorry; it's not very heroic, is it? Do you hate me?' I looked at her fearing her reply.

'Oh, Phil!' We were still in an embrace. She looked deep into my eyes from a distance of less than six inches. My heart skipped several beats. Then she kissed me, pressing her lips against mine in an ardent, long smooch. Maybe it was my imagination, but I could have sworn that there was an orchestra playing somewhere, and were those fireworks?

CHAPTER TWENTY-SIX

Love Lost... and Found?

It turned out that Elise had, reluctantly, been forced to keep some things from me. One of the things she hadn't told me was that, at their last communication, Dr Gold had given Elise a contact number. It occurred to me that Dr Gold had expected something like this to happen. I kept that to myself.

'I wanted to tell you, Phil, but I was sworn to secrecy. If I was captured, or you were, and anyone knew I could contact her, they could try and get the contact information out of me, or worse, you. Then Dr Gold herself would be in danger.' Elise was hugging me, and her voice was a little uncertain. She must have thought I would be upset by not being told everything, but I was just happy to be with her and have her holding me like this. I was happy to let her have secrets and her spy stuff. As long as there would be times like this.

We were back at home now, my home. Elise had brought me back after everything had been sorted out.

Elise had made her phone call, from the Russian safe house to Dr Gold, and within a couple of hours, there she was in her magnificent Jensen Interceptor. This was my favourite car of all! I watched the car draw up and I drooled. Out of the driver's side, stepped Dr Gold's driver and bodyguard, the woman we had spoken briefly with at the end of the phone. She introduced herself as Celestine. She was easily six feet tall and looked strong and capable, with an automatic pistol in a holster strapped to her hip. She was also a very attractive woman, with a rather voluptuous figure. She shook hands with both of us. I looked up at her as she shook my hand, and my mouth dropped open in admiration.

'Put your eyes back in!' murmured a voice next to me. 'Don't you know it's rude to stare.' I blushed for shame, but as I took a sly glance at Elise, I could see she was trying hard not to laugh. She took my hand and squeezed it. As we waited to talk to Dr Gold, a large van drew into the drive, marked 'Silver and Gold Cleaning Company Ltd'. It sat on the driveway, no one got out. It seemed they were awaiting orders.

Celestine stared at the damage done to the house by our gunfire. She whistled softly. She reconnoitred the place thoroughly, inside and out, before she was satisfied it was safe to let Dr Gold out. She went to the door of the interceptor and opened it for her distinguished passenger to alight. Immediately, Elise snapped to attention. She was quite a sight, in her dark clothes, with shoe polish on her face, criss-crossed with the tracks of her tears, and smeared where she had tried to wipe those tears away; nonetheless, as she stood there, proudly erect, she made a dignified figure. Pride and love filled my heart. So, not to be left out, I stood at attention too. I heard a snort of laughter from my left. I ignored it.

Dr Gold approached us. She beamed at Elise, then, to my astonishment, she swept Elise into her arms and hugged her tight.

'Oh, Elise, the things you've been through, and what you've achieved! I had no idea of the perils I was putting you in.'

Elise looked rather startled too, but she recovered and accepted the embrace. 'Thank you, Aunty,' she gushed.

I turned and gaped at the two of them. Had I heard that right? Was that something else Elise was keeping secret, even from me? She turned to me and winked, as if to say, 'I'll tell you later.' I snapped my head back to face forward once more.

'I couldn't have done any of it without Mr Lavender here,' Elise consoled, then turned and gave me a warm and affectionate smile. 'He saved my life at least four times.'

I wouldn't have minded a hug from this rather attractive older lady, but she contented herself with a warm handshake.

'I think we can dispense with pseudonyms for a

while, don't you? What is your proper name, Mr Lavender?'

'Erm, Ph-Phil, Philip W-Williams.'

'Well, Mr Williams, Philip, if I may. You have really done something exceptional. Something to be proud of. Thank you for saving my niece's life. I can say that now, now that she has given the game away...' at this point, she gave Elise a hard stare. 'She promises to be an excellent agent, but she is precious to me for other, obvious reasons. Leave your address with her and await something exciting in the post.'

She waved to the people waiting in the van, and they came out. About six people altogether, they started to clear away the trussed-up Russians lying around here and there. They took especial care of the former Mr Plum. After they had gone, and Dr Gold had finally taken her leave, Elise and I sat in the big house on a settee holding one another.

'I'm so sorry, Elise.' I held her, and rocked her as she had once rocked me. 'I know you love him.'

'He used me!' she spat. 'I think you can take it that any love I had for that... that *rat* is over!' There were tears running down both our faces again. Weeping seemed to be a feature of our relationship at this time. I always thought love would be a happy thing, joyous, walking on air, etc., but for the past few days it had been so painful, and so much heartache.

'I really loved him, and all the time he was using me.'

I didn't know what to say, so I stayed quiet and hugged her.

'Why didn't I just shoot him dead, Phil? I wanted to!'

'You know why. You were too professional. And I love you for it.'

'No, actually, it was thinking of you that stopped me.'

'Really?' I was surprised.

'That and the thought that we needed the information from him.'

'Ah!' That was Elise, when it came down to it, she was professional to her fingertips; fingertips that were currently entwined in my hair.

I learned later that Mr Plum soon gave way under interrogation. He did not believe in communism particularly, he just liked money, and he was being well paid for betraying his country. So, there were no ideological reasons for him to keep quiet. He gave names and details of his contacts to Dr Gold and her team, and the process of rolling up the Russian network began.

Ken had pretended to be captured and beaten up, just to gain the trust of the young trainees. It turned out that he had been involved up to his neck in the capture of Elise's teen team. He was the one who had sent the Russians to capture Elise that first night, and the other trainees.

There were really very few in the conspiracy, but

it included people who were very high up in the British secret service, and these people *were* committed communists. They were called sleepers, and they had worked their way up in the service, while all the time supplying information to the Russians. They were still in the process of gathering information about the teen spy programme and had, by a stroke of fortune, not yet sent their final report to their spymasters in Moscow. So the programme was safe, at least for the time being.

Elise was going to go on being a spy, and in a private, 'most secret' little ceremony, she was given the result of her final assessment – the spy equivalent of A*, a medal and her credentials. I was allowed to be there as her plus one. It took place in an unassuming civil service office in London.

Dr Gold was as good as her word. In the post a few days later, I received a beautiful certificate, a medal, and a cheque for an eye-watering amount of money. Enough to see me through university, and a little way beyond. This was a little harder to explain to my parents, and I was forced to tell them some of the truth, although not all of it. I told them I had helped Elise by stopping some men from beating her up one day. Which was true as far as it went. I told them Elise was training to be a civil servant, and the money was part of a reward scheme set up by the civil service to protect their employees.

When I realised that I was quite good at coming up

with these little stories, I decided to study creative writing at university.

Did Elise and I have that holiday? You bet we did. We went skiing that winter, and I was able to give my 007 fantasies full rein, while I was learning to ski. Elise, of course was an excellent skier.

— EPILOGUE —

The secret agent breathed in the pure alpine air, feeling it filling his lungs, cold and invigorating. High up here in the Austrian Tyrol, the powdery snow was deep and fresh. Just right. He paused at the top of an incline, beside a grove of pine trees. Down below he could see his quarry. After observing her for some moments through his Zeiss binoculars, he launched himself over the brow and down the slope. The wind blew back his black hair as he schussed confidently down the mountain. Dressed in his Bogner stretch ski pants and matching jacket, the secret agent looked a million dollars. So did his target, in her Christian Dior powder blue top and salopettes.

She caught sight of him, stopped and waved. As she stood waiting for him, her red hair riffled entrancingly in the breeze and her lovely mouth smiled, revealing perfect white teeth. She waved a greeting and leaned on her ski poles, showing off her excellent trim figure. He could imagine her green eyes sparkling behind her Ray Ban sunglasses. He performed a last parallel turn and a hockey stop that brought him to a halt right next to her.

'Hello, Elise.'

'Hello, Mr Lavender. There's trouble,' she said, casually. 'You're needed.'

'But there's no train out of here for three hours.'

'Oh my,' she replied, raising an immaculately plucked eyebrow. 'What are we going to do around here for three hours?'

Splat!

Elise reached down for the hundredth time that day and helped me to my feet.

'You know,' she began, and smiled. 'I actually think you're improving. You stayed up for almost a minute that time!'

I spat out the snow from my mouth, looked up at her and grinned. With her help I struggled to my feet.

'Hot chocolate?' she asked. I nodded, and hobbled alongside her, holding on to her arm as we walked on up to the hotel.

The End